Love Me, GOALTENDER

4 Horsemen
Publications, Inc.

4 Horsemen Publications, Inc.
1497 Main St. Suite 169
Dunedin, FL 34698
4horsemenpublications.com
info@4horsemenpublications.com

Typesetting by Niki Tantillo
Cover by 4 Horsemen Publications, Inc.
Editor: Sienna Skye

Library of Congress Control Number: 2021951210

Paperback ISBN-13: 978-1-64450-455-0
Audiobook ISBN-13: 978-1-64450-453-6
Ebook ISBN-13: 978-1-64450-454-3

To anyone and everyone who believed in me, even when I didn't. You keep me going.

Table of Contents

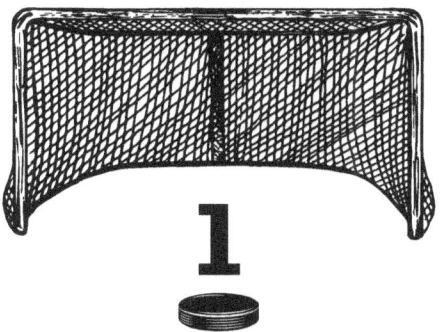

1

I stared up at the Snow Globe Arena as if I hadn't practically grown up in the place. I had been inside the walls of the hockey arena countless times over the past twenty-one years. Almost every home game during the regular season, my family and I were in the stands, cheering on the New York Blizzards. It was my home away from home, and I was finally back.

Except I wasn't walking through the big, arching entrance at the front. I was taking the players' entrance because I was the New York Blizzards' first female goalie.

Okay, I realized I was being a little dramatic. Hell, I had already been inside the stadium this morning to sign my contract and for morning skate, but it was finally happening! I was going to play my first NHL game. After spending my rookie year riding the bench with the Seattle Blades and barely setting foot on the ice, it was looking like I would be doing the same this season. Then I got traded to New York, and not just any New York team—the Blizzards. I held in my girlish shriek.

A car alarm beeped, followed by the sound of a grumbling man-child. Ah, right, the reason I was staring up at the building and not entering it.

"Come on, Mason," I shouted, my breath puffing out in the chilly air.

Mason shot me a withering look as he grabbed his backpack and slammed the back of his neon green Jeep closed.

"Hold your fucking horses, Riley. And don't call me that," he yelled back.

While he slowly got himself together, I took a quick selfie in front of the sign and sent it off to my brother. Drew hadn't been to the stadium in years. We'd stopped going to games after the plane crash that took our parents away five years ago, but now that I was part of the Blizzards, he was coming back. He wouldn't miss my first time starting for anything.

Just as I was about to say, "fuck it" and ditch Mason, he caught up to me, backpack over his shoulder, sipping his coffee, and looking nowhere near as excited as I was.

Since my car was still in Seattle, I recruited Mason as my reluctant chaperone. But had I known waking him from his nap two hours ahead of his regular schedule would be like dragging a corpse across town, I would have just taken a cab. The guy looked like he was about to keel over, but that may have had something to do with him trying to follow my mad dash from his car to the doors. Mason didn't like to exercise when he didn't have to. Ironic, for a professional athlete.

Not willing to wait a second more, I grabbed his arm and towed him toward the entrance reserved for players and staff. Two guards opened the doors, and the arena underground unfolded before us. The large concrete tunnels bounced dozens of echoing voices across the space. I shivered at the blast of warmth, happy to escape the freezing February air, and clenched Mason tighter.

"Shit, Riles. I know I'm not the best player on the team, but we really don't need another injury right now." He shook his arm. I loosened my grip but didn't let go. He had a point; Blizzard players had been dropping like flies lately. The only reason I was traded was because Travis Hall, the Blizzards' backup goalie, tore his ACL.

I smiled up at him. "You're totally right. You're not the best player."

He snorted and wrestled me off him. "Rude," he said, but his dimples flashed with his perfect smile. He looked out of place in the chilly New York weather. With his sun-tanned skin, longish brown hair with light highlights, and sparkling green eyes, Mason was your stereotypical Californian surfer boy. Except for the fact that he had never been to California nor touched a surfboard in his life.

Security wanded us and our bags as we passed, heading toward the locker rooms. "It's weird being back here with you," I said as I took in the tunnels for the second time today.

"I know. I feel like we're kids again. Do you remember that day?"

"Of course. New York vs Colorado. Goss made that beautiful diving save against Brockovich in the second. It was gorgeous." Damn, just remembering it gave me chills. I hadn't even gotten close to stopping a shot that legendary in my short career, but that was going to change. And soon.

"What? No, you asshole! When we met."

I snapped back to reality and smirked. "Oh. Yeah. That was good too."

Mason socked me in the arm playfully, and I scrunched my nose at the sting.

We *had* met that day. Midway through the first period, I wanted a closer view than I had from my family's box. So I escaped and ran down to the rink, where I found a twelve-year-old Mason with his face smooshed against the glass. I joined him, and when the period ended, I took him up to our suite for milkshakes. By the time my mom called his, apologizing that I kidnapped her son and inviting her up to join us, we were best friends and there was no separating us.

After I found out we were the same age, I abandoned my pee-wee hockey team and made the hour trip to the Bronx three times a week to join his. Then, with a little help from my lawyer parents, I transferred to his middle school, and we had continued our careers and lives together ever since. That was until we got drafted to different cities. I went to the Seattle Blades' farm team, and Mason got to stay home in New York to play for the Blizzards.

But Lady Luck was on my side, and I was back and ready to kick ass.

I followed a step behind Mason as we made our way through the circular hallways. The tunnels down here were confusing, even after the short tour I had been given this morning by management. We took a left at the 1962 team poster, and the players' lounge entrance appeared.

I stopped before the lounge doors like I had at the arena entrance a few minutes ago and earlier this morning. "I don't think I'm ever going to get used to this. I thought my star-struck days were over with my rookie season. But..."

Mason chuckled. "It's just because it's our home team. Go on, take a picture. You know you want to."

"Not with this many people around."

We looked around and caught the eyes of more than a few people.

"Right. You're still a novelty," Mason said under his breath and raised an eyebrow at an arena worker whose gaze didn't flick away from us fast enough.

As much as Mason was used to playing with me, women were still new to the NHL. Rachel McCarthy, Vancouver's backup goalie, had only joined the league four years ago, breaking the glass ceiling on her way and opening the doors for the rest of us. I was drafted to Seattle's farm team a year after her and called up the next season, but no other women had been selected the past couple years. And as I hadn't been on the ice for more than fifteen minutes since I was drafted, progress was slow-going.

So, as acclimated to famous hockey players as the stadium workers were, I was still a rarity. I could feel their eyes tracking me from the moment I walked into the building. But I was used to it, and shaking off the discomfort, I swiped my newly acquired ID.

I smiled politely at the staff as we made our way through the large space, past the lounge and food areas, and into the main locker room. The room was circular, with several dozen wooden cubbies around the perimeter. It was pristine and blissfully empty. And then I saw it.

I couldn't hold in my squeak this time as I ran, avoiding stepping on the team logo in the middle of the floor, to the cubby that had a freshly pressed sweater hanging in it. "Warren" stretched across the shoulders in black, my lucky number 88 sitting dead center. They hadn't had it ready this morning, so it was the first time I was seeing my new uniform. It was like I was a rookie all over again. It was the same name and number from Seattle, but they looked infinitely better affixed to this new blue-and-white sweater instead of my old green one from the Blades.

I dropped my small duffle bag on the seat and touched the sweater in reverence, and Mason laughed behind me.

"Really, Riles?" he asked.

"Yeah. Here. Make yourself useful." I tossed him my phone and posed beside the sweater, a smile tugging at my face and a peace sign thrown up.

Mason shook his head and took the picture. "Damn, I missed you, girl."

"I missed you too. FaceTime is just not the same."

Mason returned my phone and watched over my shoulder as I sent the photo to my brother for when he had service again. "Is Drew here yet?" he asked.

"He should be landing soon. He said he didn't want to get here too early and distract me before the game. As if he could. You coming home with us tonight?" I tossed the phone into my cubby and kicked off my heels. They followed my phone, and I silently bemoaned their loss. I loved dressing up on game days, and those heels were fierce.

"Is Drew cooking?" Mason asked as he wandered over to his cubby a few slots away, already drawing his jacket off. I turned my back to the room and copied him, taking off my slate grey pantsuit in a few seconds, leaving me in only my bra and panties.

"Yep, making *kasha* and cabbage rolls."

"Then I'm there."

"We're going to the store after the game to get ingredients. And some vodka to celebrate if we win or cry into if we lose," I called over my shoulder and undid my bra.

Mason gagged audibly. "If you make me drink that gasoline, I'll cry no matter what."

I laughed. The first time he tried the vodka from my mom's stash, he spit it out immediately. When she found out, my mom was so mad that we wasted her good Russian vodka that she didn't even care about the underage drinking. "It might be good. Everyone needs a good cry now and then."

"True. Shit is cathartic, man."

The new voice came from Ethan "Tank" Jones as he came through one of the side entrances into the locker room. Even hunched over his phone, he certainly was a tank, with shoulders just as broad as he was tall and able to plow through a horde of forwards with little to no effort. I hadn't met him this morning, but he had been Mason's mentor when he was first drafted, and Mason talked about him often. Apparently, he was an extremely hard worker. He would have to be—it was hard to be a minority in the NHL. Ethan Jones was the first black team captain of the Blizzards. He was also the nicest man on the ice.

He wasn't the one that grabbed my attention though. Sebastian Kingston followed a step behind Jones. While he was slightly smaller than Jones, he filled the room with his very presence. Sebastian "The King" Kingston was the team's star forward and was one of the best scorers in the league. He could shoot from almost anywhere on the ice and was a force to be reckoned with in the speed department. After he was drafted to Dallas in the first round at age eighteen, he busted a ton of rookie records and was crowned "The King." The first season after he was traded to the Blizzards, seven years ago, he won the team the cup. He was a legend.

I had seen him in person several times and on hundreds of hours of game tape. Just like on the ice, he stood rod-straight, head angled up like he was perpetually looking down his slightly crooked nose at his subjects. The nickname fit him. All that was missing was a crown atop his wavy black hair as he met my stare, his grey eyes hard. Then those eyes dropped to my chest and almost popped out of his head. His pale face turned ashen. "Uhm."

I looked down. I was mostly naked. Whoops.

"Holy shit," Jones' exclamation brought my head up, but I kept my face completely blank.

With deliberate nonchalance, I stepped backward into my cubby area and tugged the curtain that ran on a curved rod around only my locker closed. Silence reigned as I pulled on a sports bra and a pair of leggings. You would think the guys had never seen a pair of tits before. But they had better get used to it. As much as the curtain concealed, there were going to be some nip-slips; it was inevitable.

While I was offered a private room to dress in this morning, I turned it down like I had when Seattle offered the same. Nudity didn't bother me much, and the cons of having a separate room weren't worth any discomfort I might feel. In high school, I had to have a separate dressing room as it was a liability issue for the school. Vancouver was the first to put in the curtains when they drafted Rachel McCarthy. The NHL offered separate dressing rooms to McCarthy, of course, but being close to your teammates to bond was essential when your gender already divided you. A curtain in the dressing room and separate shower areas were the best solutions for concealment while still being as close to the rest of the team as possible. Seattle and New York followed Vancouver's lead when I joined their teams and added curtains. Although they had a couple flaws, like me not remembering to close them. Especially when it was just Mason and me; I'd been naked in front of him so many times, I barely even registered him in the room when I was undressing.

And now I had just met my captain and assistant captain tits first. Great. If they had been at the optional practice this morning, this wouldn't have happened. I zipped up my new team hoodie with a huff.

"Oh, Captain, my captain," Mason crooned at Jones. "Finally managed to get to the rink? You weren't here earlier for morning practice, so I figured an old man like you was spending the day in bed."

Sufficiently dressed, I opened the curtain, grabbed my shoes, and sat down. Thankfully,

Jones was leaning against his cubby, taking Mason's cue to act like nothing had happened. Kingston, on the other hand, had tensed at the sound of the curtain tracks and had yet to relax, his traps stiff by his ears as he stared into his locker, his back to the room.

"Me and Kingston had a media thing to do. And of course, I'm here. Couldn't miss seeing Warren out there tonight." Jones turned to me. "I hope you don't choke your first time starting, Warren. Frey here, has hyped you up a lot. Although, from what I've seen of you, I'm not sure if it's warranted."

Jones' bright smile softened his harsh words. Instead of being offended, I smirked and chirped back. "I don't choke. Ever. But I *am* a little worried about everyone else. Are you sure the pressure won't get to you? You haven't had this many eyes on you in a while. Can *you* handle it?"

Mason burst into laughter as Jones sputtered. "Okay. Wow. Confidence."

"Trust me, guys," Mason said through his laughter. "Riles is unfazeable."

Sebastian finally turned from his stare down with his locker. His intense gaze landed on me. He obviously doubted Mason's statement.

"I guess we'll see if that's true in a few hours," Jones said, echoing the sentiment in Kingston's eyes.

I held Kingston's stare without a flinch as I answered Jones. "I guess you will."

11

Kingston cocked a single eyebrow then turned back around to start undressing. I averted my eyes politely.

"Well, you got Mason here early. You're already a miracle worker in my eyes," Jones said.

"Hey! I haven't missed a practice in three seasons—optional or not," Mason defended himself, but I could see the playfulness as he bantered with Jones. Mason had not been excited about having Jones as his mentor his first year. But after weeks of listening to Mason bitch about Jones' "try-hard bullshit advice," his complaints reluctantly turned to thinly veiled compliments. Seeing them now, I could tell how Jones won his fellow center over. He was a natural captain—charismatic, friendly, and full of positive energy.

I couldn't fathom why the Blizzards' management tried to give the job to the cranky asshole undressing in the corner, even though he had the best stats on the team. I was grateful for whatever reason had Kingston turning down the captain position years ago when Armstrong retired. I couldn't imagine him with the C on his sweater.

The sound of a door opening pulled me out of my musings, and I sat up straight as Coach Hansson entered.

"Frey, what are you doing here? Shouldn't you be napping somewhere?"

Jones laughed in triumph, and Mason groaned. "Riley needed a ride, Coach."

"You don't have a car, Warren?" Coach asked.

"It's on its way from Seattle, but I'm in no rush. Not when I have my own chauffeur."

"Fuck you, Riles. See if I give you a ride home tonight," Mason chirped.

"So, no *kasha* for you?"

Mason froze. "I take it back."

"What's *kasha*?" Jones asked.

"It's a Russian dish," Coach Hansson answered before I could. I cocked my head at him.

"You cook, Warren?" Jones asked, not looking surprised that Coach knew what *kasha* was. Coach wasn't Russian as far as I knew. How did he know what we were talking about?

Mason scoffed at Jones' question, and I raised a middle finger preemptively. Mason didn't disappoint. "God, no. Well, not Russian food, at least. Her mother was never able to beat it into her and, after three kitchen fires, stopped trying."

I rolled my eyes. He was exaggerating. It was only two kitchen fires. The last one didn't count—I put it out before it left the pan. I was about to point this out to Mason when I saw the cringe on Sebastian Kingston's face. Jones and Coach had the same look. Right. Dead parents made people uncomfortable.

I exchanged a look with Mason, who had realized what he said, and shrugged. Whoops.

Coach coughed. "Warren, I need to have a quick word. Do you have a second?"

"Yes, sir. I was just about to find a quiet place to meditate."

Coach nodded. "I can show you to an empty room. Come with me."

Glad for a chance to escape the deathly—ha—silent room, I strode after Coach.

I had only briefly met Hansson earlier at morning skate, but he didn't say much to me past the standard "welcome to the team." I didn't expect to be intimidated by him, but as I watched him stand in front of the team, giving instructions, he seemed like a mountain. As a woman who regularly stared down two-hundred-pound men that wanted to send a puck through her face, that was saying a lot.

Hansson was one of the league's best centers in his time. He was an unstoppable beast with swift feet and a brutal backhand. That was until Corey Schroeder rammed him into the boards during the second game of the 1985 Stanley Cup finals and permanently fucked up his leg. Rather than let that injury end his career in hockey, he picked himself up and became a coach. Now, twenty-something years later, after making his way back up to the NHL, he was the Blizzards' terrifying head coach.

He led me out of the locker room and took a right. He didn't say a word. I followed and waited.

We came to a stop outside of a nondescript door, and after peeking inside, Coach flicked on the light and held the door for me.

I walked into a small box barely long enough to lie down in. It must have been a janitor or supply closet at one point. The Blizzard blue walls and the grey carpet looked new. A single light bulb hung illuminated from the ceiling. Hansson closed the door behind him.

"Is this a good room for you to mediate in or whatever?"

"Yes. This will do. Are you sure no one is using it?"

He waved his hand dismissively. "No. You're fine."

"Thank you."

I waited. He looked at me from his spot at the door. I leaned against the wall behind me.

"What's up, Coach?" I kept my voice light.

"Warren. I'm sorry to do this, but I have to know. Are you serious about this? About playing on this team? In this league?"

I didn't hesitate. "Are you?"

His eyebrows scrunched. "Am *I* serious?"

"No. Are you sorry? You wouldn't ask any other player this. I understand that you feel this is necessary. But are you *actually* sorry?" I crossed my arms. The man was like a drill sergeant, something his buzzed dark hair and permanent scowl only enhanced. I met his eyes softly—not challenging him, but genuinely curious.

He paused, eyes drifting to the side, and I appreciated that he took his time to think before answering. Then he faced me, and I saw the formidable center he was decades ago. "Yes. I am. I am sorry for what I have to do. You're not a rookie, I know that. But you've never played a game at this level before. I need to know if you're going

15

to crack under the pressure. So"—he pushed off the door—"are you serious about this? Are you going to go out on that ice and push yourself to your limit, or is this just a fun game to you? Because we're not going to make it easy. You're not the first woman in the league, but you still have to prove yourself. Rachel McCarthy did on her team, and now it's your turn. You are the only other woman drafted since McCarthy. You'll have to show the world that she wasn't a fluke. Can you do that?"

I dropped my hands to my sides, stood up straight, and added some weight to my stare. "Coach, I love hockey. I love it more than anything. Trust me, I'm under no illusions about how hard this is going to be, but I want to play. And no amount of bullshit will stop me. I'm not going to let anyone down. I can't. So let me go onto that ice and prove to you that I can handle anything. And prove to the world that Rachel McCarthy is not an anomaly."

Coach considered me. "What about the press? This job is more than just the game on the ice."

I waved him off. "I know how to deal with the vultures. I'm a gay woman in a traditionally male sport. If I haven't been driven out of the game by now, I don't think I ever will be. I can take it from the press. I can take it from the fans. Hell, I can take it from my own teammates. I have before, and no doubt, I will again. As long as I get to be on the ice out there, I can take it all." It was a good speech, even with the little lie thrown in.

Hansson slowly nodded, and I saw something impossible—his lips twitched. Then his face broke out into a huge smile. "You know, I was against signing you. I wasn't sure if you were worth it. If you could handle the punishment. I truly hope you can back it up and surprise us all."

"Oh, I can, sir. And by the way? This *is* just a fun game to me. That's why I won't quit. I like having fun."

"Well, hot damn. Sounds like a plan to me. I'll let you get ready now. See you on the ice."

He left, and I stared at the door as it closed behind him. Hansson had a soft side, who would have thought?

I turned off the lights, settled onto the carpet floor, and practiced the breathing my therapist taught me years ago, shaking off any thoughts that didn't have to do with winning a hockey game.

*I*t took a few hours to finish my pre-game routine, but when I was done, I was fully ready to kick ass on the ice. After my meditation and visualization, I warmed up with some stretches and did a few coordination drills that consisted of a bunch of tennis balls and a now scuffed-up wall.

Most hockey players—and athletes in general—had specific routines before games. Goalies were infamous for having the most extreme ones. While mine wasn't as precise as, say, Braden Holtby's, it was necessary. My mind tended to stray before games, and a routine tells my brain that it's time to forget everything outside the rink and stop some pucks.

Loose and excited to play the game I loved, I danced to my music as I went in search of a stationary bike, needing to kill some time and stay warm until it was time to hit the ice. Mason was in the hallway outside the gym playing soccer with a few teammates. I waved at him and shimmied by, avoiding the curious faces of my new teammates.

The large gym was set up into two areas—a padded warm-up area to the left and exercise machines to the right. I circled the gym, ignoring stares from the half-dozen players in the room—three were on bikes, a couple on treadmills, and the last mid-pike stretch on the warm-up mat. I plopped onto a clean spot on the mat and ran through a few stretches. Already stretched out, I only did a few cursory exercises before getting up. There was a free bike in the corner, but before I could claim it, a faint sound cut through my music and drew me up short. I tugged out my earbuds, pausing the music, and faced the man who had entered the gym and called my name. Oh, great.

"Riley Warren. Nice to meet you. I am Alex Lukin," Lukin greeted me excitedly with a strong Russian accent.

I paused at his enthusiasm. Teammates were never that nice to me, at least not when we first met. Lukin would have even less reason to be nice to me. He was the Blizzards' starting goalie. I was his rival.

About the same age as me, Lukin was called up as a backup for Travis Hall when Blake Stanton, the starting goaltender, got hurt. Then Lukin became the starting goalie himself when Travis Hall was taken out of the game a week later. It was the fastest promotion ever, and while

I would never wish injury on another player, the weird circumstances got me and Lukin into the NHL. But I doubted Lukin was as excited as I was about me being here.

I shook his offered hand warily. "Nice to meet you too."

"You here to stretch?" he asked and cocked his head, his blond hair flopping into his eyes. It was startling how much he looked like Drew. With his classic Russian looks—blond hair, blue eyes, and a strong jaw—he looked more like my mother than I did. While Drew got our mother's Russian genes, I got my father's brown eyes and had to bleach my hair to get it the platinum shade of blonde it was now.

"I just finished. I'm heading to the bikes." I jutted my thumb at the row of them. He nodded, a pleasant smile on his face, and said nothing. I raised my eyebrows and moved to step around him.

"Do not worry about game. I will go stretch and be ready to take over when you give up." *There it is.* I almost sighed in relief. Assholes, I knew how to deal with. Nice guys, not so much.

Lukin's smile turned poisonous. I shot him a sugar-sweet grin in return. I liked that he saw me as a threat. He should. I walked away without another word.

"*Pizda*," he spat at my back in Russian. *Pussy.*

"*Nu, ty to, chto ty yesh'*," I returned, making sure my pronunciation was perfect, and didn't look back. *Well, you are what you eat.*

I wished I could have seen his reaction, but as I got onto a bike, my neighbor, Erik Berg, a veteran defenseman, snorted in amusement, obviously having understood us. Lukin stalked out the gym door.

It seemed Lukin was pure-blooded Russian, homophobic and sexist—the winning combination. And the top reasons that I had never visited Russia.

My mother had always wanted to take Drew and me to show us where she was born, but by the time we got around to going, Drew and I had both come out of the closet and Russia was not safe for us any longer.

Thankfully, Mom didn't have the same hang-ups as Lukin.

I replaced my earbuds and pumped up P!nk, starting my bike and shaking off the negativity. It wouldn't faze me. Not today.

"Okay, boys, settle down," Coach called the team to attention. The rap music was quickly shut off, and the guys quieted. I caught the tennis balls I was juggling and tucked them away.

We had just come off the ice from our warm-up and were sitting in the locker room, getting pumped up for the game. I struggled to keep myself under control and not let my excitement overtake me. The tennis balls helped me focus a little and ignore any distractions, but I wanted to skip all this bullshit and just get onto the ice.

I took some measured breaths. We had a few more minutes before the game started.

Everyone sat at their designated lockers. The once spacious room was much more cramped when filled with a couple dozen guys, fully decked out in hockey gear. Especially over in the goalie corner. I sat in my cubby, sandwiched between Lukin and the half-wall by a side entrance. Having nowhere else to go, our bulky leg pads invaded each other's space. I was surprised my pads didn't disintegrate where they touched.

With the team's attention, Coach Hansson quickly recapped the game plan for today. We were playing the Pittsburgh Piranhas. They were top two in the eastern conference and were on a massive winning streak. They were a tough team and had already beat the Blizzards bloody a month ago as our team had been struck with a bit of an injury problem amongst its players. It was going to be a rough game. A smile crept up on my face just thinking about it.

Coach finished talking logistics and went silent. Everyone waited.

"It's going to be an interesting game tonight," Coach said. "All eyes are going to be on us. Don't let it sike you out. You know what you have to do. We are here to make this team the best it can be, so do your part and your very best. Good luck."

I stared at Hansson. That last part seemed oddly directed at me, but I couldn't tell how. I looked around the room but could only meet Mason's eyes, everyone else staring at Coach or at the floor.

Hansson clapped. "Okay, let's get this done."

The team stood as one and whooped. I gathered my gloves and mask.

"Good luck," Lukin snarked as he pushed around me.

I narrowed my eyes after him. Taking one more deep breath, I centered myself, pushed back some blonde strands that had escaped my braid, and slipped on my mask. It was go time. I stepped to the front of the line forming at the rink entrance, grabbed my stick, and led the team through the dimly lit tunnel.

I only had to wait a moment before the team was announced, and I rushed onto the ice, my team following. We took a few laps around, and I stared at the audience in awe.

The arena was packed to the rafters, the overwhelming amount of white and ice blue making the rink look like our team's namesake—a blizzard. Dozens of signs rose above the crowd. Held by more women and girls than I had ever seen at a hockey stadium at once, the posters were decorated with my name or number. I couldn't believe my eyes. Rachel McCarthy had something similar for her first game but seeing it in person, instead of through a television screen, was a whole different experience.

It was amazing, but as I flew past the crowd, a pang shot through my heart. The seats were in section D, right behind the glass. I didn't have to look hard to find them; they drew me toward them. But they were filled with the wrong people.

Instead of the faces of my parents, a strange family dressed in Blizzard's blue and white cheered. The mother had a little girl in her arms, and a teenage boy sat to the father's right. It was like looking into a time-warping mirror.

I scooped up a stray puck from the ice and, on my next lap around, threw it to the family that wasn't mine.

The whistle blew, and a puck was dropped into the ensuing fray. Two sticks jabbed at the rubber disk, fighting for the upper hand. The Piranhas won, and a red-clad forward charged down the ice, his team flanking him. My team followed at a leisurely pace.

Damn it.

The red figure and his teammates triple-teamed me, the puck passing between three sticks like a pinball. I couldn't keep up. A stick ripped through the air, and less than ten seconds into my first NHL start, a puck sailed into the net behind me.

The blaring goal horn buried my curse, but the audience didn't let that stop them and, after a brief pause of confusion as they tried to understand what just happened, erupted. The boards surrounding us shook as fists rained down on them. The yelling and cursing that spewed from the crowd was terrifying, and I was glad it was directed at my team instead of me. They deserved it.

To their credit, they didn't try to defend themselves. Our starting line stood in the middle of the ice, where they hadn't moved since the initial fight for the puck, and accepted the boos and hissed curses from the crowd. It was the consequence of betraying their fans.

The players on the bench were getting the same treatment. Hundreds of people were screaming. Someone threw a drink over the boards and into the benches. A few of my teammates looked nervous at the backlash, but none of them glanced in my direction. At the end of the bench, Mason looked over our team with disgust.

Even the referees didn't know what to do.

The only person who met my stare was Coach Hansson, his arms crossed, trapping his clipboard.

"Are you sorry?" I mouthed through my mask.

His chin lifted, stubborn and as unmovable as the rest of him.

"What the fuck?" an accented voice asked in confusion.

Right. The Piranhas. Five opposing players stood around my net, looking shocked and a little petrified at the noise. They hadn't even celebrated their shot. Pierre Babin, the French right winger who dumped the puck through my legs, skated up to me.

"What is going on?"

"Oh. Don't worry about it, Babin. It was a good shot, but you should go back to center ice. We've got a game to play." I kicked the puck out of the net and smiled at him sharply but toned it down when he winced. Maybe that grin was a little too crazy. Unfortunately, I had a feeling I would need the crazy for the rest of the game.

Babin and his team skated back to where my team was getting back into position. There was no need for a line change after such a short play. Jones took the face-off position, the Blizzards spreading out behind them, and I wondered if they were going to actually help this play. They kept their eyes on the ice. I scoffed.

As if he heard me from across the ice, Kingston looked up from his position and caught my gaze, his grey eyes as icy as the rink below our feet. His face was stone, unapologetic, and I recognized the look from the times I'd seen him play and from the hours of game tape I'd watched, studying him. Just like Coach, he wasn't flustered in the slightest. It looked like I would be fighting two hockey teams tonight.

I arched an eyebrow through my mask and smirked at him.

Alright, you little bastards, bring it on!

It was a brutal five minutes, but I was holding steady at an impressive four pucks in and eighteen stopped. Admittedly not what most NHL goalies would call impressive, but I think I had the right to call extenuating circumstances. The boos from the crowd hadn't put a dent in Coach Hansson's resolve, and the first period continued with me facing down every Piranha play almost entirely by myself. My team only helped with the occasional steal, minimal defense, and half-ass skates toward the Piranhas' goal. They didn't usually get far before a Piranha stopped them, stole the puck back, and then came at me. What was worse, I was pretty sure the Piranhas were going a little easy on me; I hadn't been triple-teamed in three minutes. God, my opponent felt sorry for me.

I took a much-needed water break as the teams switched shifts and set up the next face-off.

"Come the hell on," Mason screamed from the bench and slammed his stick against the boards. He hadn't set foot on the ice yet—no doubt Hansson's doing. From Mason's reaction earlier, he had no idea what the team was planning. I knew if he had, he would have told me. Unfortunately, Hansson seemed to know that too. To stop him from going rogue and stealing the puck, he had been effectively benched.

I smiled and returned my water bottle to its place atop the net. At least one person was on my side.

The crowd echoed Mason's anger. Well, okay. Maybe more than one person had by back. I could only imagine what my brother was screaming somewhere in the stands right now. Knowing Drew, it wouldn't be pretty.

I settled into my crease and locked eyes on my rubber target.

How our team managed to accidentally come up with the next puck, I don't know. But it was quickly stripped from them, and once again, I was facing down a Piranha breakaway. I shimmied in the net with anticipation.

Surprisingly, my team followed and tried to steal back the puck. With every new play, my team tried a bit harder to act like the professional athletes that they were. But as it was, with them mostly on lack-luster defense, I felt like I was a kid playing with a bunch of puck-shy toddlers.

Jones managed to move his ass in front of the puck, but Russo, the Piranha center, shot it between his legs. Across the ice, Babin came up with the puck and headed my way. A quarter down the rink, with no one between me and him, Babin shot with no hassle. No hassle for *him*, at least. The puck took flight. My glove raised to meet it, but it curved at the last second and headed for my face.

The tiny rubber disk deflected off the side of my helmet, the force blowing the straps off my mask and sending me stumbling into the post of the net. I caught myself before I could collapse and locked my knees. Like hell was I about to show weakness.

I breathed through the hellish ringing in my head and rolled my neck. Luckily, the puck didn't hit me head-on. It was just a light graze. Even through the finishing of Beethoven's Fifth in my ears, I could tell that the crowd had fallen silent for the first time since the beginning of the game. I dropped my glove and felt around my mask. Everything was intact. I could keep on playing. But the sound of frantic skates pierced through the ringing, and I looked up to see the starting line closing in on me.

"Woah, woah, woah." I held up my glove-less hand to ward them off. "I'm all good, guys. Honestly."

"You sure?" Jones asked, his brow furrowed. That was unexpected.

I glanced around, and sure enough, the rest of the team had similar expressions. Even Kingston was looking me over carefully. On the bench, the team was standing, half a second away from launching onto the ice. A team doctor came rushing to the rink door. I caught his eyes, made a slashing motion across my throat, then gave him a thumbs up. There was no need for medical attention. The ringing was already almost gone.

"I'm fine," I answered Jones truthfully and eyed him curiously.

"Uh, okay." He fidgeted, shifting on his skates, his concerned face becoming sheepish.

"Are you mad, though?" Ian Decker, a defenseman, asked with a wince.

I tried not to laugh in his face and only half succeeded. I was more pissed about the puck than anything they had or hadn't done. "Are you kidding me? This is the most fun I've had in years!"

From the looks on their faces, they were questioning my sanity. I chuckled again. I was basically playing against a professional hockey team all by myself! Who else can say they've done that?

I shooed them away. "Go on."

They dispersed, all but one going to the face-off circle closest to me. Ethan Jones veered to the bench and had a quick, quiet talk with Coach. When they broke up, Jones joined the rest of his line.

I reattached my face mask straps, put on my glove, and got back in the net.

It was on the next puck drop, lucky number twenty-one, that our captain went to work. Jones stole the puck and flew across the ice, Blizzards in tow. The Piranhas were as stunned as the crowd by the team's sudden activity, and their hesitation allowed for a Blizzards' breakaway.

Poor Charlie, the Piranha goaltender, didn't stand a chance. The puck bounced between Jones and Kingston until they decided to stop playing with their prey, and Kingston slammed the puck into the goal, the net billowing with the impact.

Our goal horn blared.

Well, would you look at that.

Their celebration was thankfully tame—a simple high five. The confused crowd mumbled. A few whoops came from the back, but most of the home crowd didn't seem inclined to forgive them just yet.

Coach called for a line switch, and on his way off the ice, Kingston caught my eyes and gave me a nod.

I adjusted my pads and deepened my squat. It looked like the game had finally started.

With the help of my teammates, the score was 2-4 by the end of the period. *Better late than never, I guess.*

The team trudged into the locker room silently. Words were unnecessary at this point.

Following the team inside, I stopped to get a bottle of Gatorade and a granola bar before taking my seat in the quiet locker room. Overheated, I stripped off my sweater and upper body pads. I didn't think I had ever sweated this much from a single period of play.

I chugged half my drink in one breath then started in on my snack, aware of every eye on me but not caring.

Mason, who had been glowering the entire period, even when he was put in after the team started trying again, stomped over to me. "Move over," he growled at Lukin. Either out of fear or because of seniority, Lukin obeyed, and Mason took his seat, pissed-off expression still in place. Aww. My savior.

Mason wasn't stupid; he knew what was going on. We have been playing together since we were preteens. He knew the shit I had to go through; he was there for most of it. He had just hoped his current team was above it. I knew better. He nudged my shoulder in solidarity, and I smiled around my granola. It was us against the world just like always.

"What just happened?" Henry Nicks, a rookie, asked a couple seats away. He must not have been briefed before the game.

"It was a test," Mason volunteered when no one else answered. Uh, oh. His Bronx was coming out, his tone leaving no question about how irritated he was. Half the gazes in the room turned to the floor uncomfortably.

At Nicks' still-confused face, I finished off my granola bar and filled him in.

"They wanted to make sure I was worth all the bullshit they're about to go through. You must have seen the news coverage around Rachel McCarthy. Breaking *one* glass ceiling comes with consequences, but two? Rachel and I are not only the only two women in the league, we're also the only out queer people. I got a ton of shit in Seattle even though I barely stepped onto the ice. Now here in New York where I'm a fresh face and actually starting games? The media is going to be on my *ass*. It's going to be a goddamn circus, but if I flaked out on the first game and quit, it would have been a non-issue. Hence a test. Judging by the sudden desire to act like fucking professionals after I got grazed, I'm guessing I passed?" I shot the last part toward Coach Hansson, who had been leaning against the whiteboard the entire time.

He gave a nod.

Then for the first time since I "met" Sebastian Kingston, he spoke to me. "Yeah, you're worth it. Now there's just one question—do you think *we* are worth it?"

I stared at him for a second before the laughter burst out of me, uncontrolled and genuine. Kingston raised an eyebrow, the other one joining it as Mason's low chuckles blended with my slightly hysterical giggles.

"Do you really think that you could make me quit this game?" I asked through my shaking. "I've been proving myself my entire life, bigshot. This little cold shoulder act of all of yours is the least of my worries. Right now, you should focus on taking back the game. If you can, Your Majesty."

The tension shattered, and a few of the guys broke into good-natured "ohhhs" as Kingston's face cracked with a tiny grin. Huh. I didn't think his face did that. The grey eyes that had been so cold earlier, sparkled with a hint of playfulness.

Coach clapped to grab our attention. "Okay, boys and girl. Let's get back out there."

The rest of the game went by a lot smoother. I allowed in two more goals in the second period, but I didn't let it stop me and shut them down in the third. Our offense, on the other hand, wasn't able to take back the win, unsurprisingly. All things considered, the 4-6 loss wasn't too bad. And the hometown crowd agreed.

We received standing applause as we shook hands with the Piranhas. Babin even apologized for the accidental headshot. The team was in good enough spirits considering our loss as we entered the locker room, talking and jeering with each other.

Sweaters and pads started coming off immediately as players wandered back to their lockers.

Coach didn't have much to say. He would have known his antics in the first period would cost him the game.

"Okay. We've got Friday off, so I'll see you on Saturday. The vultures are waiting outside, and as much as you hate them, no one deserves to smell you all. Go shower. I will be getting my ass handed to me by our feared owner. Good luck with the evil scavengers. Give them hell."

3

*T*here were many reasons I was grateful not to be the first woman in the NHL. Near the top of the list was the shower argument. When Rachel McCarthy was drafted, there was a huge argument about locker rooms and showers. Obviously, women couldn't shower with the guys, but you couldn't remove the women from the locker rooms either because bonding is invaluable for teams. Shutting women out of the space where most of that bonding was done would have been detrimental to the team dynamic. The curtain worked in the locker room, but for the showers, the Vancouver Talons built Rachel a personal shower in their players' lounge. Desperate to be inclusive in the eyes of the public, the rest of the NHL followed suit and constructed separate shower areas in all home and guest locker rooms for any future women joining the league.

The women's showers were not as big as the men's, but with the full space to myself, I had more than enough room to rinse off the rough game. After patting dry, I wrapped my hair up in a towel, slipped on my bra and panties, and went to join the boys.

The locker room was a mess—sweaters strewn everywhere and pads shoved haphazardly into cubbies.

I got to my locker and didn't bother with the curtain. My important bits were covered, and everyone had been avoiding looking in my direction all day anyway. Not that teammates tended to look. There was always locker room etiquette, whether it was all guys or there happened to be a woman on the team. The most basic rule is simple—don't stare. Get your shit done as fast as possible and try not to make anyone uncomfortable. In my experience, most players in the NHL stuck to that. No doubt they got a lecture from management before a woman joined the team. They didn't look at me, and I returned the favor. It was professional courtesy.

But Lukin didn't know how to be a goddamn professional.

"Nice," he said with his strong accent, leaning against his cubby wall, and ran his eyes over me. I could practically feel them leaving a slimy trail on my skin.

Not looking at him, I stepped into my slacks and shoved my arms through my blouse.

"I mean on ice. You did nice job."

Sure, that's what he meant. I buttoned up my shirt.

36

My silence must not have been entertaining because, after a few moments, he stalked off with a huff. Hopefully to wash off that smell. Coach wasn't kidding; we reeked.

Fully decent, I turned around, and as I suspected, no one else was looking my way. Lukin, however, should take a few pointers on how to not be a fucking creep. It might help him if he didn't want to get bitched slapped sometime in his life. Whether that slap would come from me or somebody else, I didn't know. I just hoped somebody recorded it.

Across the room, Mason came out of the showers in a cloud of steam, towel wrapped around his hips, and went to his cubby. I scrubbed my hair dry as I waited for Mason to slip his underwear on beneath his towel then joined him. He didn't even have to look up to know it was me.

"I'm still pissed at them," he grumbled softly as more players emerged from the showers. "I lost a lot of respect for everyone, especially Jones and Kingston. They're usually against rookie harassment. The next time I see Babin, I'm going to punch him in the face."

"Honestly, I'm surprised you didn't jump the bench when I got hit." Mason was a mother hen at heart, but I was grateful that he'd kept it together. He knew I could take care of myself and that I wouldn't want him to embarrass me in front of the guys. If he had, I wouldn't have taken it well.

"I thought about it for a second, but I didn't want the next person hit to be me. You've got a wicked right hook, and I can't ruin my pretty face right now."

"Of course, you can't." I leaned in and lowered my voice. "Not when Drew is here."

He recoiled, and I laughed.

"Fuck you," he grumbled shyly and ran his towel over his head, the freshly showered fluff of brown hair undercutting his bitching. He was a fucking puppy, and I couldn't resist scrubbing my hand through his hair.

"Ugh, no. Get off." He slapped at me, and I dropped my hand.

"But honestly, Mase, it's fine. Well, not really, I don't like it either, but just drop it. The quicker everyone gets over this, us included, the easier it will be for everyone. I just want to play hockey. And Babin didn't mean it. He already apologized."

He huffed and finished getting dressed into his game suit and coat.

"Come on," he said. "Let's get out of here. I need food."

We stopped so I could get my heels, blazer, coat, and bag from my cubby then left the locker room.

We walked directly into a horde of reporters. It was like a zombie movie, and I was the last human on Earth. They descended on me.

Mason got pushed away as they formed a tight semi-circle around me, each holding a microphone, phone, or camera. Lights flashed in my face. I didn't bother fighting back my irritation and gave them all the stink-eye. Fucking vultures.

The first question that broke through the noise was an easy one.

"Riley, how was your first start in the NHL?"

I didn't know who asked, so I directed my answer to the group at large. "It was tough. I thought I was ready. I've watched a lot of games and spent a few minutes on the ice in Seattle, but nothing prepared me for playing a full game in the big show. The play is on a whole other level. It takes a lot to keep up with all the guys out there, but I think I did an okay job." A perfectly adequate answer.

"Are you disappointed that you lost your first game?"

"Sure. I'm an athlete. I'm competitive. It always sucks to lose, but it gives you a lot of motivation to try even harder next time." I knew what they were hedging around, and I wasn't going to make it easy on them.

"How do you feel about your team leaving you in the lurch at the beginning of the game? That was a shitty thing to do."

Well, at least someone had the balls to say it straight-up. It didn't mean I was going to give them the emotional reaction they wanted, though.

"I wasn't stoked, but I understood why they thought it was necessary," I deadpanned.

"Have there been any negative comments made toward you?"

"No." My answer, like my attitude, was short and clipped. They were buzzing around me like flies, and I wanted a swatter.

"Stanton and Hall are going to be out for the rest of the season. Do you think you or Lukin will become the next new goalie for the Blizzards?"

"You would have to ask management about that."

"Are your teammates' wives mad that you're in the locker room with them?"

I didn't bother answering that one and looked over their head, grateful for the extra inches my heels added. Mason was leaning against a wall, texting. Damn it, Mason. I wouldn't have minded a rescue now.

"Do you have a girlfriend?"

"I'm not going to answer anything that doesn't have to do with hockey." *Buzz off.*

The door swung open behind me, and I shuffled to the side as much as I could. The ambush of journalists had made me block the lounge door.

"What the fuck is this?" a voice growled behind me. He had barely said two sentences to me, but I already knew his voice.

"Kingston," a reporter shouted into my ear. "Is Warren's presence a distraction on the team? Is that why you didn't help her during the first minutes of the game?"

He looked down at me with his hard, grey eyes and took my wrist. "Come on, Warren, you've got to go see the trainers before you can leave," he announced and dragged me through the crowd. The vultures didn't follow as he hauled me down the hallway.

I waited until we were out of earshot. "The trainers are in the opposite direction."

He released me and shrugged. "I know."

I opened my mouth to question him more, but before I could get anything else out, we were interrupted.

"Riles," Mason called as he jogged up to us. "Sorry. I didn't think you needed help."

"I didn't," I denied instinctually then paused. I turned to Kingston and softened my tone a bit. "But I appreciate it."

He nodded.

"Warren! Frey!" Jones came bounding from the direction of the lounge. "You guys coming out with us tonight? We're meeting up with some of the Piranhas at Satan's Place, a bar a few streets away. You gotta celebrate your first official game in the big leagues, Warren!"

"Satan's Place?" I raised an eyebrow.

"You don't have to drink if you don't want to—half of us don't. But there's good music and a chill vibe."

Mason waved him off. "Sorry, Cap, we can't. It's a family night."

"With you?"

"He's part of my family," I answered. We could go and just bring Drew along to the bar, but I didn't want to. Just because I understood why they did what they did, didn't mean I wasn't a little salty about it.

"Geez, man. Give her a second. I'm sure she wants some time alone to throw darts at our pictures," Kingston said, and I saw the impossible thing again—Kingston's grin. His eyes crinkled with mirth, and I noticed a light scar carved through the corner of his upper lip and into his stubbly cheek.

"Oh, right. Okay, see you guys later." And off Jones went.

"Thanks," I muttered to Kingston. He had saved me from another awkward interaction.

The scar on his lip twitched with another grin. "No problem."

I stared after him curiously as he left.

"Come on." Mason nudged me, oblivious to my momentary lapse of brain function.

I quickly shook off whatever trance I was in, and Mason and I found our way to the parking lot, where my favorite person in the world was leaning against Mason's lime-colored Jeep.

"Heads up," he yelled and whipped his arm in a blur. I caught the fuzzy, yellow ball seconds before I ran and crashed into him. He squeezed me and spun, my feet dangling in the air. With all his layers on, it was like hugging the marshmallow man.

"Nice game, kid!" Drew set me down and patted my head like I did to Mason earlier. "Good job."

Arghhh. I pushed him away and karate chopped him.

He defended against me, turned to Mason, and pointed. "And you."

Mason put up his hands in surrender. "I did what I could."

"Hmm. You know where Jones and Kingston live, right?" At Mason's nod, Drew continued. "Perfect. I say we hunt them down and kick their asses for being dicks to Riles."

"No." I threw the tennis ball back at Drew. It hit him in the chest, but he managed to catch it on the rebound and tucked it into a pocket of his jacket. "You can't fight everyone who doesn't like me. Also, have you seen those dudes? They would crush you."

"Um, excuse me. Have you seen these muscles?" Drew flexed his arms.

"What muscles? You're an accountant." In truth, he did have some impressive biceps. Not that you could see them through the million layers of clothes he was wearing. For all his Russian looks and the fact that he'd lived in New York his whole life, Drew hated the cold.

"I am not an accountant. I'm an investment banker. Plus, I wouldn't do the heavy lifting. That's what Mason is for."

I laughed. "Mason hasn't even thrown a punch on the ice yet."

"Hey," Mason chimed.

"How about Mason doesn't punch anyone tonight." I turned to Drew. "And instead of you being an accountant or investment banker or whatever, you be a chef."

"Oh, I like that plan," Mason said.

"Fine," Drew conceded. "But we need to stop and get ingredients."

"Yeah, I have nothing at the house. Did you drive here?" I asked. Drew shook his head. "Then hop on in. Let's get out of this cold."

We got into Mason's Jeep and went in search of food.

Drew had inherited the Upper West Side brownstone when our parents died and finished raising me there. It was our childhood home, and even when we both left New York for work, we couldn't bring ourselves to sell it. It just felt wrong. Now that I was back, Drew was going to sign the deed over to me. The thought was surprisingly painful.

"Don't think you're not helping me cook, Riles. Only Mason gets to sit on his pretty ass," Drew called out as he unlocked the door and walked inside as if he had done it every day for years. It was still a struggle for me to walk over the threshold.

I breathed through the feeling and carried the groceries into the kitchen.

"Did he just call my ass pretty? Is my ass pretty?" Mason whispered behind me, more bags in his arms.

I rolled my eyes and laughed. "How would I know?"

"Oh, please. You're not a real lesbian. Is my ass pretty?"

"Hey, I'm mostly a lesbian," I said even as I internally cringed. I still felt guilty about lying to the world about my sexuality, but the alternative wasn't fun. And, ideally, if I end up with a woman, it wouldn't be an issue. Not that that was going to happen for at least a few years. I didn't have time for a relationship, not when my career was finally taking off.

"Just tell me," Mason whined quietly as Drew dug around in the cabinets. Mason and I set our bags on the counter.

"Fine. Yes. You've got a big ol' bubbly hockey ass. Now take it over there and leave me out of your sexual tension with my brother." I pushed him away and unpacked the groceries.

Having two lawyers as parents didn't allow much time for home-cooked meals, but my mother always tried. She would cook *Paskha* or *Solyanka*, trying to remember her mother's old recipes from Russia. She didn't always get them right, turning out more than a few inedible dishes. But when she got it correct, she got it perfect. It was how she kept her culture alive in herself and in her kids.

The *kasha* and cabbage rolls didn't take long to prepare. Mom would always make them after my games, and when she was gone, Drew took over. They were healthy, filling, and comforting—perfect for game days.

After we all quickly changed out of our suits, Drew designated me as the official chopper as he puttered around the kitchen, ingredients flying around him in a controlled tornado. I dutifully sliced the vegetables and didn't stab Mason when he stole bites. Little gremlin.

It took more than a little fumbling around, but the cabbage rolls and *kasha* came out more or less authentic.

"Wait for them to cool," Drew warned when Mason got too close to the rolls on the counter.

"But I'm hungry," he whined like the man-child he was.

"How about some drinks while we wait?"

Mason watched with horror as Drew cracked open the new bottle of vodka. "Oh, dear God."

"Yes," I cheered and retrieved the cranberry juice from the fridge.

Drew scrunched his nose. "A real Russian does not sully good vodka with fruity crap."

"Yeah, well, I don't want to wake up outside again. So…" I flipped him off with one hand and grabbed the vodka with the other.

4

The hulking figure sped toward me from the middle of the ice, a puck flittering off the lightning-fast stick and bouncing around the blurring skates. He was coming left. Then right. No, it's left.

I pushed off my skates to intercept, but the puck disappeared. Where... There!

I dove to the right. There was no time to get my blocker up. I sprawled on the ice, and the puck slammed into my chest pads. Air burst from my lungs.

I flopped onto my back, dropped my glove, and pulled off my helmet. The ice cooled my sweat-slicked hair. "Ouch."

Mason laughed and retrieved the puck from where it bounced off me. "And it's Warren with the sacrifice block," he announced, his voice booming around the empty practice rink. Then he crouched, looking down at me. "You know this isn't the cup finals, right?"

I heaved myself to my knees, and Mason stood to give me a hand the rest of the way up. I adjusted my pads and shot him a smirk. "It's worth it to keep your ego in check. Can't have you thinking you're too good."

Mason snorted and skated off to the bench. I followed, chuckling. All hockey players have some ego. Every athlete does—they have to in order to perform. But compared to all the other professional athletes I've met, Mason was the least egotistical. He was the true embodiment of a team player—never taking credit for his team's work and doing everything in his power to make sure he was friends with his teammates. And with a personality like his, everybody loved him.

Unfortunately, the same can't be said for me. For the entire year and change that I was on the Seattle Blades, I didn't make a single friend on the team. It was partially because of the nature of a goalie—the position being the most solitary one on the ice—but it was also because I didn't try. There was no need to; I had tried making friends with my male teammates for years, and the outcome was always the same.

"Well, my ego isn't the thing that's bruised here, is it?" Mason raised an eyebrow at me.

I grimaced and snagged my water bottle, refusing to rub my aching chest. The puck had caught me right in the tit. I didn't think it would bruise, but it was definitely sore. Unlike Mason, I wore full pads for practice, but pucks still hurt. I flipped him off in retaliation, but he didn't notice, looking over my shoulder.

"Kingston," Mason shouted suddenly, almost making me choke on my water.

I spun around, wiping the water from my chin. Just outside the practice rink, Kingston looked up from his phone. He stood still as Mason skated up to him. I followed behind at a slower pace, stopping to pause the music on Mason's phone.

"Do you wanna join us for some extra practice," Mason asked.

On the other side of the glass, Kingston looked just as shocked at the offer as I felt. Damn Mason and his desire to be nice to everyone! Just last night, I was holding him back from hunting down Kingston, and now he invites him to join our practice?

"I'm sure he's busy, Mason," I said, giving Kingston an out. He didn't like me, and I was sure he didn't want to spend extra time with me. I shouldn't want to spend time with him either.

Kingston paused, and just when I thought he was going to politely decline, he grimaced down at his phone then looked up again. "Yeah, I could use some more ice time."

"Of course, you could," Mason said with a laugh then turned to me. "I swear this guy spends more time in rinks than you."

That was saying something. The ice was my happy place, so every chance I got, I was on the closest rink I could find, stopping pucks or just skating around.

49

"I was basically born on a rink, bud. Let me grab my stuff, and I'll be right back," Kingston said and took off.

The second he was out of view, I turned and socked Mason in the bicep.

"Ow. What was that for?"

"Didn't you want to kill him five minutes ago?"

"Eh, I mostly wanted to kill Jones. Besides, Kingston's not actually the asshole you think he is, and you need to make friends on the team. I love you, Riles, but it's not just you and me. You have to build relationships with our teammates. You never did in high school or last year, and how did that turn out? You need to get the team to like you and to want to work with you. If you get Kingston on your side, the rest will follow. He may not be the captain, but his opinion carries the same weight as Jones'."

I huffed at his reasoning and skated off to gather up the stray pucks. Logically, I knew he was right. Team bonding was extremely important. Hell, that was the reason I made a point to stay in the locker room with the guys, but just being together in a confined space wasn't enough.

Mason joined and helped me herd the pucks into a pile at center ice.

"Come on, Riles. You've already proved what you can do. What you can take. Trust me, after that headshot you took, everyone is more than a little impressed with you."

I smiled at that, and Mason continued. "Now it's just politics. This game isn't only about skill;

you know that. You have to build a rapport with the guys. Get them to like you, and you've basically got a permanent spot on the team."

For the surfer-dude image Mason projected, he did know his shit. And there was nothing I wouldn't do to stay in the NHL and on the Blizzards.

"Okay," I conceded and went to turn the music back on to get rid of the funk that had invaded my mood.

I was dancing circles around the rink when Kingston came back, dressed in team-branded athletic attire, his arms filled with gear. Like Mason, he didn't bring his full pads. I stopped skating and joined Mason at center ice as Kingston sat on the bench, tied up his skates, slipped on his gloves, then joined us on the ice.

"Why are you guys out here anyway? It's our day off," Kingston said as he skated around the rink to warm up.

"It's relaxing, and God knows Riles needs the practice," Mason said.

I rolled my eyes and grabbed a puck with my big goalie stick. I waited for Kingston to come closer on his next lap and shot the disk across the ice. Kingston received it smoothly and added some impressive stickhandling to his light warmup.

"What about you?" I asked. "Why are you here? Nothing better to do?"

Kingston joined us, pushed his tousled hair out of his face, and gazed down at me, eyes shining through his dark lashes. "I had a PT session, and I needed a little workout."

I nodded, suddenly distracted. Damn, his eyes were pretty. I made a mental note to not get too close to him on the ice during an actual game. The last thing I needed was to be struck dumb in the middle of a play.

Thankfully, Mason interrupted and brought me out of my daze. "We're just shooting and blocking today. We didn't want to drag out a bunch of equipment for anything else."

I skated to my crease as the boys got ready and slipped on my mask.

Thirty minutes later, I ignored the sweat dripping into my vision and kept my eyes glued to Kingston as he zigzagged up to me, reading his every eye twitch and anticipating his next move. His stick flowed smoothly around him in a simple but hypnotizing dance with the puck. It looked to be a straight-forward approach, but as I slid backward into my net, body shifting with the puck, a flash of silver stole the puck from my sight. Suddenly, Kingston's stick was ripping through the air, and chasing the slight glimpse I caught of the black circle, I lunged to the right. The puck dinged off the corner of the left post and ricocheted into the net, leaving me empty-handed and empty-headed.

What? I peeled myself off the ice, still staring at the puck in disbelief. Kingston skated around the back of the next then headed casually toward center ice where Mason stood with his jaw hanging open.

"What the hell was that?" I demanded, sliding from my crease, leaving my glove, blocker, and stick behind. As I got closer to Kingston, I stripped off my mask.

Kingston shrugged in his usual noncommittal manner.

I swept a fly-away out of my face and chewed on my lips as I thought. That was some of the best footwork I'd ever seen. He'd effectively turned his skates into two more sticks, bouncing the puck off his blades. It was as smooth as a soccer player dribbling a ball, so fast and flawless that I couldn't tell how many times his skates had redirected the puck. It could have been once, twice, or even three times.

"That was awesome," I gushed. "But I'm pretty sure I've never seen you use that in a game before."

Kingston nodded. "Yeah, it's not perfect yet. Maybe in a few more months."

"I think it's good to go now," Mason said in disbelief. I agreed.

Kingston shrugged and snagged another puck. He didn't seem nearly as enthused as he should be. That shot was fucking impressive. How long had he been working on that? If I were him, I would have been doing enough cellys to get carded right now. Kingston fiddled with the puck as he waited for Mason to take his turn at me and the goal.

"Is that you, Warren?" a voice suddenly called over the ice.

We all turned to see Coach Hansson standing by the rink entrance.

"Hey, Coach, you need me?" I asked, already heading toward him.

"Yeah. You too, Kingston. I was just about to call you guys, but someone mentioned you were already here. We need to talk real quick." He gestured for us to join him.

I looked back at Mason and Kingston for answers, but their matching confused looks told me they had no idea what was going on either.

We glided across the ice and stepped onto the rubber mats outside the rink door.

Mason shifted on his skates.

Coach spared him a glance. "Give us a minute, Frey."

Mason's eyes flicked to me. I shrugged. Without further ado, Mason followed the rubber mats to the locker room, balanced perfectly on the thin metal of his skates.

Kingston sat on the nearest bench and took off his gloves. I stayed standing in the door of the rink, fiddling nervously with the mask in my hands. Kingston plucked at the tape on his stick and waited for Mason to disappear before talking. "What's up, Coach?"

Hansson crossed his arms over his chest and stared at the top of Kingston's bent-over head. "I need you to bring Warren to your charity event after our next game."

Kingston's head whipped up. "What? Why?" He echoed my thoughts exactly.

"Because you're her new mentor," Coach Hansson said casually.

I met Kingston's eyes, confusion and dawning horror bouncing between us.

Fuck. I so did not need a mentor. If they would just give me some time, I could figure everything out on my own. It wasn't like I was a rookie. Granted, I hadn't played a full game with the Seattle Blades, but I still held my own on the team and with the media. If I ran into anything new on this team—which I doubted—Mason would be there to help me out. He'd done it before. I didn't need Kingston, a guy I didn't know, to take me under his wing.

"Why not Frey?" Kingston said, and I jabbed a finger at him in agreement. "He would be happy to mentor her."

Exactly! Mason was my person. And I didn't want to be an annoying weight on Kingston's shoulder. The guy was undoubtedly busy. With the new skills he showed during our little practice, he must have been working to improve constantly.

Besides, with Mason being my childhood friend, he was the most obvious choice.

"Not that I need a mentor at all," I cut in, slightly irked at not getting in a word yet in a conversation about my own career. "I grew up in this city, and I'm not exactly a rookie."

Coach turned to me. "Aren't you? Yes, you've been in the NHL for a year, but last night was your first start. All things considered, you did very well. And based on your performance, I think you're going to do well on this team. But you need a mentor to show you how to work with your teammates. I've talked to your old teams. You don't play well with others."

If Coach wasn't directly in front of me, I would have assumed that it was Mason giving me the same lecture he had been for the past few years.

"So, Kingston's going to show me how to make friends?" I deadpanned.

Coach shrugged. "Basically."

Fantastic. Mason is going to love this.

Kingston tugged off his skates and stood. "Again, why me? Frey is a thousand times more amicable than I am."

Coach waved him off impatiently. "Frey is too green. If they weren't injured, I would have assigned Stanton or Hall and let them all bond over their weird goalie shit. But they're out right now, and I saw the way you helped her with the press last night. I think you two are a good fit."

Kingston grunted, and I eyed him skeptically. Why would Coach think that? Kingston barely spoke to me. Even during our short practice, he only spoke when spoken to.

"Take her to your charity event on Sunday, and get to know each other," Coach continued. "You never know; you may grow to like each other."

Kingston grimaced at Coach.

I held in my huff and tried to act like an adult. "What kind of charity thing are you doing?" I asked Kingston with the least amount of attitude I could manage at the moment.

"I coach," Kingston said shortly.

"It's with kids," Coach interjected, and I perked up in interest. "Your Seattle PR manager said you volunteered with kids a lot, Warren."

"Yeah, as much as I could," I confirmed.

Kingston's head whipped to me.

In Seattle, I volunteered and donated gear for kids who wanted to play but couldn't afford to. The thing about Hockey is it's hella expensive. Skates and pads cost hundreds of dollars, and then you have to get new ones whenever you hit a growth spurt. It was rough on people financially, and I tried to help where I could. It was the one thing I hated about leaving Seattle. I didn't get to see the kiddos anymore.

"That's perfect. Sebastian donates pads and skates to kids and runs drills with them when he can. You can tag along and maybe teach the tiny goalies a thing or two."

I softened a little. I didn't know Kingston did that. He didn't really seem like the kid-friendly type. I was surprised they didn't run screaming from his gruff face. He could be a scary bastard, especially on the ice.

57

"They probably need some help. I doubt Kingston could teach a brick wall how to stop a puck," I teased Kingston, and he shot me a narrow-eyed look. *See what I mean? Scary bastard!*

But then Kingston's hard face fractured, and he threw me a tiny smirk. "I could stop any of your shots."

I snorted. "That's not saying much. A two-year old could shut me down." I'd tried offense a couple times over the years, not thinking it was that hard. It was. I couldn't get a single shot past Mason. He still gave me shit about it, but I've threatened him with bodily harm should he tell anyone else about my failures.

"So, you'll take her with you, Sebastian?" Coach asked.

Kingston stood from the bench. "Yeah, she can come. I'll get a kick out of watching a bunch of pre-teens wipe the ice with her."

I fought the urge to stick out my tongue like a pre-teen myself. On the inside, I cracked a smile. Kingston seemed, if not pissed, not entirely put out about me joining him.

"Great." Without another word, Coach left, no doubt eager to escape in case we changed our minds.

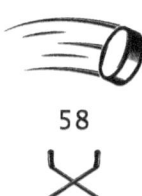

We were silent as we gathered the pucks and dumped them into a bucket. Then we grabbed our things and made our way to the lockers.

"So, my new mentor, huh? I bet you wish you hadn't stayed to help us practice now," I teased, determined to keep the tension at bay as we wobbled our way across the rubber mats.

Surprisingly, Kingston shrugged. "Ehh, you're not so bad, Warren, and I enjoyed the distraction." At my raised eyebrow, he elaborated. "My girlfriend bailed on me."

"Oh? A *girl*?"

"Yeah, a girl." He didn't sound enthused.

"Must be a pretty special one to get Sebastian 'The King' Kingston to leave the rink."

He raked a hand through his hair. "I think the extra time at the rink, the workouts, and the practices are the problem. She doesn't really like my hours and gets annoyed when I spend more time away from her than I'm required to. You know how it is."

I nodded. I *did* know how it was. I struggled to date in Seattle, and I wasn't even going to try to start a new relationship now until I get myself established on the Blizzards. With the way Coach and Mason were echoing each other, bonding with my team needed to become my top priority. And I had a feeling this season would have enough drama without adding another person into the mix.

"Why are girls so weird and complicated? I've dated a lot of women, and just when I think I've got them figured out, they completely change. This chick, Sarah, we started dating, and she loved that I was a hockey player. She used to come to all our home games and team events, but now she's complaining about my hours as if she didn't have a problem with them a month ago. I think I need to break it off with her."

I had to take a second to recover from the shock; I'd never heard him talk that much uninterrupted. I shrugged off the astonishment at his tiny speech. We reached the locker room, and I held the door open for him. He gave me an amused look at the action but stepped through.

Inside, Mason's things were in his cubby, but he was nowhere to be seen. The muted sounds of running water came from the showers. Kingston sat down to untie his skates, and as I faced my locker to strip off my pads, I couldn't help but take advantage of the empty room, my curiosity pecking at me. "How long have you been with her?" I asked, keeping my back turned to the room as I threw the last of my upper body pads into my cubby. I was down to my leg pads and skates.

"Almost eight months now."

I spun on my skates. Kingston was sitting in his cubby, his skates laid next to him. Copying him, I sat down in mine and shook my head. "Really, bud?"

"What?"

I unlaced the last of my pads and skates. "You've been together for eight months, and she's only now getting serious? You should count yourself lucky she held off this long."

"Getting serious?" He cocked his head to the side, and I fought the urge to pat his hair like I did with Mason and Drew when they were being stupid men. Then it struck me; Kingston and I were in this same position not even a day ago, but now, instead of glaring at each other, we were having a heart to heart.

I tugged off my skates, contemplating. Maybe making friends wouldn't be so hard after all.

"Yes," I said. "Getting serious ... well, she was probably already pretty serious. But it takes a minute for men to catch up sometimes. It's alright, you got there eventually. Mostly." I finally freed myself from my pads and was unencumbered by anything but my undershirt and leggings. "Look, hooking up with an athlete is fun, but we're hard to date. We have crazy schedules, and we care about the game more than our partners usually do. If she wants you to spend more time with her than you do at the arena, she's ready to get serious. Serious enough to have a say in your career and your life—marriage serious."

Understanding filled his face, then apprehension. "But we're not even living together. It's way too soon to even start thinking about rings."

I shrugged. "You're saying you don't know anyone in the league who got married to someone they knew less than a year?" Because I knew more than a few. Athletes had high-stressed, fast-paced jobs, and our relationships tended to be just the same.

Kingston must too because his face soured. "How do you know all of this?"

I pointed at myself. "Girl who dates girls." That was enough explanation, even if it was carefully worded. Technically, it wasn't a lie.

"What's this about lesbians?" Mason asked as he barged into the room, dripping wet, with a towel around his hips. I jolted backward into my cubby. I hadn't even noticed the water shutting off. Instead, I had been leaning forward as if I was trying to get as close as possible to Kingston while still staying across the room.

"Just thinking how much easier it would be if I were gay," Kingston joked bemusedly. "At least then I would understand my partner. It must be so much easier for you to be a lesbian, Warren. Especially in the NHL." He stood, turned to face his cubby, and stripped off his shirt.

Behind his tattooed, muscled back, Mason and I exchanged matching shocked looks. Kingston's little throw-away comment was way too close to home.

Mason coughed out a fake laugh then changed the subject. "So, what did Coach want?"

I thumbed at Kingston, who was organizing his things. "He's my new mentor. Apparently, he's supposed to help me make friends since I need them or whatever."

Mason was just as taken aback as we had been. "What? Seriously? Coach said that?"

Kingston turned around with an eyebrow raised at Mason's incredulous tone.

I grimaced at what I knew was coming.

"Ha!" Mason cheered. "I've told her the same thing a dozen times, and Coach agrees with me!"

I rolled my eyes. "Yes, you're amazing, Mase."

"I know. You should listen to me all the time."

"Oh, go dry off and leave me alone."

Kingston watched our back and forth with his usual flat expression. Then a smirk flashed across his face, faster than lightning. "You should also take a shower," he said to me.

I took a sniff of my clothes and reeled back. "Oh, damn."

I was about to playfully chirp back about pots and kettles when Kingston faced his locker again and dragged down his boxer briefs. I saw a glimpse of toned ass and calmly, respectfully, faced my locker. Seconds later, footsteps disappeared into the showers.

"You want me to wait for you?" Mason asked somewhere behind me.

I cleared my throat and forced out a neutral tone. "Nah. I'll see you later." My car had gotten to the city that morning, and I drove myself to the stadium. Mason was officially free from chauffeur duty.

As Mason scrubbed dry, I said goodbye to him then headed for my own shower.

Other than a missing Mason, the locker room was the same when I came back from my shower. Despite him going to wash off before me, Kingston's things were still in his cubby, and the sound of water was coming from the men's showers.

By the time I got mostly dressed behind my curtain, the shower was still on. Was he shaving in there or something? I'd taken shorter baths.

I finished dressing in some leggings and a sweatshirt then flipped my head upside down to scrub my hair dry. The cotton must have muffled my hearing because, when I flipped my hair back and stood straight, the shower was off and Kingston was walking into the locker room, eyes on the towel he was tying around his waist.

All the saliva left my mouth, and I was left gaping at him. Water slid over the hard planes of his torso and arms, shifting colors as it flowed over his tattoos.

I must have made a noise because Kingston suddenly looked up. Surprise flashed across his face as he stopped abruptly. "Oh, sorry. I thought you would be gone by now."

"I—uh—was just leaving actually," I stammered. I couldn't tear my eyes away from his torso.

Both of his arms, his chest, and the side of the torso were covered with colorful ink that blended into each other like watercolors. Short, dark lines and saturated colors popped against his skin and contoured his body. It was like someone ripped out pages from a sketchbook and glued them on him. A tingle sizzled through me, and my hand twitched, wanting to reach out and trace the details of his tattoos that I couldn't quite make out from across the locker room.

Then I remembered where I was, and I jerked my eyes away from his body, trying to save myself some embarrassment. Unfortunately, I didn't succeed; Kingston had caught me checking him out.

But instead of the smarmy smirk I expected, confusion flashed across his face.

Right. I was supposed to be a lesbian. For the past couple years, I had easily reigned in my attraction to men. It wasn't hard, considering I leaned more toward women anyway. Yet, in the couple days that I'd known him, I'd found myself sneaking more looks at Sebastian Kingston than I had at any guy in years. Now, I was straight up ogling the man in the locker room. I wanted to slap myself. I had very strict rules about looking at teammates in the locker room—namely, don't. Kingston was destroying my control, and I didn't like it.

Thankfully, there was no one else there to catch my momentary lapse of composure. I quickly recovered.

"I ... like your ink."

An eyebrow raised, he nodded uncertainly but didn't seem suspicious.

I needed to get away from him. Without giving myself time to hesitate, I threw my towel into the basket in the corner and, with deliberate calmness, gathered my things from my locker.

"Oh, wait," Kingston said, stopping me seconds before I touched the door. He reached into his cubby and pulled out a phone. "I need your number."

I rattled off the digits, and a second later, my phone dinged with a new text.

"I'll pick you up around eight in the morning on Sunday. Text me your address and bring your pads."

I barely managed a nod before I fled the room, berating myself the whole way.

5

" *S* hit," Mason cursed as his avatar was nearly sniped. He quickly turned around and ran behind some virtual trees. On the other half of my television, I watched as the guy who killed my character reloaded to take out Mason.

"Hey, watch out for that sniper," I taunted cheekily as I sipped my smoothie. My muscles, sore from this morning's workout, stretched pleasantly as I dropped my Xbox controller and stretched across the couch. I leveled out my cup before my smoothie could spill from my jostling movements.

Unfortunately, my heads-up wasn't heeded, and Mason's avatar dropped to the grass, dead. "Damn it." He threw his controller across the coffee table and onto the recliner then collapsed fully onto the couch with me, pushing my legs aside to make room for his. We watched lazily as the avatar who killed us looked for his next victim.

I checked the time on my phone. Kingston should be here any minute. I took another sip of strawberry banana. A few moments later, our avatars' murderer killed the last player and danced in victory.

Mason fetched his controller from the recliner. "Hey. Do you happen to know where Drew is?" he asked, his voice the epitome of casual, but I didn't buy it for a second.

Before I could tease him about his crush on my brother, my phone dinged. It was Kingston letting me know he was here. I stood and took my cup to the kitchen. "He went to talk to some college buddies or something. Said he should be back before I'm done with Kingston's charity thing," I shouted over my shoulder as I put the cup in the dishwasher then went to grab my huge gear bag from the hallway.

"All right. Have fun. Don't let those little kids kick your ass too hard," Mason shouted across the house.

I laughed sarcastically and would have thrown a middle finger up if he was in view. "Yeah, yeah. See ya."

Outside my house, Kingston was leaning against a white truck, waiting for me. He uncrossed his arms from his chest at the sound of my front door closing and pushed his sunglasses down from his lightly slicked-backed hair, shading his eyes from the harsh morning sun. With his black leather jacket and dark jeans, he looked like he should be dismounting a motorcycle on the cover of a men's health magazine. It was the first time I'd seen him out of athletic gear or his game suits.

I was in simple leggings and my mom's old Blizzards sweater.

"Need some help?" he asked, gesturing at the huge bag weighing down my shoulder as I jogged down the steps to the street.

"Nah. I'm good."

He nodded, walked to the back of his truck, and opened the tailgate for me. "Okay. Toss it in."

I threw my bag into the bed with the other two over-stuffed bags already in there and shut the tailgate. I kept my backpack with me and put it on the floorboard when I climbed into the passenger seat.

Kingston jumped behind the wheel but didn't start up the truck. "Is that Frey's Jeep?" he asked, pointing to the bright green car in front of us.

"Yeah. He's inside on my Xbox."

"Huh," he grunted and turned over the engine. He pulled onto the street, and I settled into my seat as we headed north. "So, you guys are really close?"

While he kept his eyes firmly on the road and his words were gruff, he was being more talkative than usual, so I decided to copy him, putting effort into this whole "friends" thing since we were going to be stuck together for at least the rest of the season. I just had to treat him like Mason. That should be easy, right? "Extremely. We met as kids and have been together ever since. He practically grew up in that house with us. He even has his own key." I snorted out a laugh. "I'm pretty sure he came over a few times while I was in Seattle just to watch tv or steal my games."

A puff of amused air escaped his nose, and I counted that as a win. I knew he wasn't the complete hard-ass I thought he was at first. He could smile and crack jokes, it just took a second for him to get there.

"It's a nice house," he said then fell silent again.

"Thank you. My brother signed the deed over to me this morning. It's officially mine, but it looks exactly the same as my parents left it. I know I should redecorate or something, but I can't bring myself to change it, you know?"

Kingston's head turned towards me for a moment, but I couldn't see his eyes behind his sunglasses. "I get that."

Damnit. Dead parents make people uncomfortable, Warren!

It wasn't like I forgot that, but after their funeral, Drew and I made a pact to mention them as much as possible. We promised not to shy away from our memories of them. We wanted them to stay as present as possible in our lives. It wasn't easy at first, and we spent a long time in therapy. But eventually, we got the hang of it. We talked about them often, not allowing ourselves, or anyone else, to forget them.

But, for Kingston's sake, I changed the subject. "What about you? Where were you born? You're Canadian, right?"

"Yep, born and raised in Ottawa."

"Oh? Do you speak French?"

The scar cutting through his stubble twitched as his lips pulled into a little smile, and I stopped myself from wondering if his eyes were sparkling in amusement behind his shades. I wasn't going there.

I couldn't.

"Not as much as my parents would like," he said

"Do they still live up there?"

"Yeah, and my sisters too. I visit them a lot. My parents still live in my childhood home. I offered to buy them a new place, but they refused. Sentimentality."

Oh. When he said he got it, he meant it.

"Do you drive?" I asked. "Ottawa's not too far from here."

"Yeah. It's about a six-hour trip. Sometimes I bring Jones with me. My parents love him."

Kingston got onto the highway, and it looked like we were headed to the Bronx. We fell into comfortable conversation about the team, me doing most of the talking, as the truck sped up the road.

Twenty minutes later, I stared out the window, watching the buildings and pedestrians fly by. I recognized the area and couldn't fight my nostalgic smile. It had been a while since I'd been back in the Bronx.

"So, what exactly are we doing?" I asked. Coach and Kingston hadn't elaborated much the other day.

"The program I partner with is for underprivileged kids. I donate and help raise money for equipment, and when I can, I join a team for practice. Today we're practicing with the Pucks. It's a pee-wee team."

Awesome. Eleven and twelve-year olds were hilarious. I worked with that age range in Seattle when I volunteered. It seemed like Kingston and I were pretty similar.

"We'll start with a warmup then do some drills," he continued. "We'll talk to them some and answer questions. Then, we play a short practice game after."

"Cool. Sounds like a plan," I said just as Kingston pulled into the parking lot of an ice rink that looked a little worse for wear. The pavement was riddled with cracks, and the grey paint on the building was faded and chipping. It wasn't anything some good TLC wouldn't fix, and I hoped the ice was okay.

After gathering our bags from the bed of the truck, we went up to the doors, but they were locked. Kingston banged on the plexiglass, making it rattle alarmingly. The doors looked a second away from falling off their hinges. Thankfully, it held.

We were only waiting outside for a few moments before I heard rushed, muffled footsteps and looked through the dirty glass door to see a middle-aged man rushing toward us.

He slipped a key into the lock and let us in. The man was sweating through his henley and was out of breath. "Sorry," he heaved out then wiped his oil-covered hand on his jeans and held it out to Kingston. "Sebastian Kingston, nice to meet you, I'm Mick Leland, the coach for the Pucks." He shook hands with Kingston then turned to me.

"Riley Warren," I introduced myself and shook his hand. "Nice to meet you, Coach Leland."

"You too, Miss. Warren." His Bronx accent was strong and comforting. He reminded me of my own pee-wee goalie coach, Coach Davidson. He was the first person outside of my family and Mason that believed me when I said I was going to join the NHL.

"I hope it's okay that Warren tagged along with me," Kingston said.

"Of course. The kids will be happy to meet you, Ms. Warren. But … we have a bit of a problem." Coach Leland turned, gesturing for us to follow him into the building.

"What kind of problem?" Kingston asked.

Coach Leland came to a stop beside the rink and turned around, a harried look on his face. "We lost power for an hour or so this morning. It came back on about thirty minutes ago, but the cooling system isn't running. I don't know how to reset it, and the owner can't get here for another hour. If I can't get it up and running immediately, the ice will start melting."

I looked out onto the ice, squinting. The surface wasn't sweating and didn't look too glossy, but the plexiglass surrounding the rink was starting to fog up. Coach Leland was right; we didn't have much time before the rink became too bad to skate on.

"Is practice going to be canceled? Or we can try to find another rink in the area," I suggested, not seeing any other solutions. There wasn't anything we could do if the owner couldn't get here in time. We couldn't exactly skate on water. Been there, tried that, almost broke my ankle for my efforts.

Leland was nodding at me, a pinched look on his face, when Kingston jumped in. "Let me take a look at the cooling system."

Leland and I turned to him in surprise. "You know how to fix an ice rink?" I asked.

He shrugged. "My parents own an ice rink, and I learned a thing or two about the equipment. I can't promise I'll know how to fix it, but I can try."

A look of hope came onto Leland's face, and he pointed deeper into the building. "I'll show you where the cooling system is."

Kingston and I dropped our bags in the stands on the side of the rink and followed Coach

Leland through a door labeled "employees only." He took us down some stairs to another door and opened it to reveal a room filled with giant, blue machines. I looked around in awe. I'd never seen this part of an ice rink before. The machinery took up more space than the entire first floor of my brownstone.

Leland pointed at a wall of metal panels. "The breakers are over there."

Kingston moved forward and popped open a couple panels. I slid off to the side, not wanting to get in their way. After a careful check of the breakers, Kingston took a quick lap around the room, inspecting the large pumps and pipes. When he was done, he came to a stop in front of us. "I can fix it," he said matter-of-factly.

"Really?" Leland asked.

"Sure. It's not that complicated. I can have it up and running in twenty-thirty minutes tops. Plenty of time to stop the rink from melting."

What the hell? Who was this guy? NHL assistant captain, philanthropist, and now ice rink mechanic?

"Great! I'll go let the owner know." Leland ran out excitedly.

Kingston immediately got to work, went up to a large panel on a machine, and poked a few buttons. I had no idea what he was doing.

"Your parents run an ice rink?" I asked.

"Yeah. They opened one up together after they got married. I helped out around the place when I was a kid, and when I turned fourteen, I officially got paid for my work. It was my only job before I got drafted." He returned to the breakers and flipped a switch. A humming started to emanate from one of the big pipes running along the walls and ceiling.

I leaned against a clean spot on the wall to watch him work. "That must have been cool. Did you get to skate a lot?"

"Yeah. I was out there every day, messing around with a puck."

I was so jealous. What I wouldn't have given to be out on the ice every day as a kid. I had tried to go to our local rink as often as I could. But as supportive as my parents were, they were both busy lawyers and couldn't take me all the time. Especially when I wanted to travel to Brooklyn to skate with Mason. Drew babysat me in my parents' absence until he was older and it wasn't cool for him to hang out with his baby sister anymore. I went less then, until Mason and I reached high school and were allowed to take the subway by ourselves, and we've dominated the ice together ever since.

"No wonder you're so damn good at hockey," I said.

He shrugged, still engrossed in the machinery. "Yeah, I guess."

"Did your parents want you to take over the rink after them?"

"God, no. Ever since I joined my first hockey team, they knew I was going to go pro. My dad told me to get onto the ice every chance I got, and it paid off."

I would fucking say. The man was an absolute beast on the ice, which made sense; he probably learned to skate before he could even walk. For most kids, going to the NHL was the goal, the absolute dream. And it seemed to come easy for Kingston. I couldn't see him being anything other than what he was. It was like he was destined to be Sebastian "The King" Kingston, but I wondered if he ever wanted to be anything other than a professional hockey player.

"Can you read off the percentage on that screen?" Kingston suddenly asked me, pointing at a reader of some kind.

I walked over, and the percentage was, thankfully, easy to find. "Ninety-six percent," I reported.

"That'll do," he said, flipped a few switches, then turned around, a satisfied smirk on his face. Huh, he hadn't even looked that proud when he got that awesome shot past me yesterday.

"You fixed it?" I asked. I had been slightly doubtful if he would be able to do it.

"Let's see." He studied a panel for a moment, then reached out and flipped a switch. The room filled with a deafening roar as if an engine had suddenly come to life.

I slapped my hands over my ear and looked at Kingston, impressed. He did it. He gave me a thumbs up.

We quickly left the room and went to hunt down Coach Leland. Finding him in an office on the other side of the rink, we told him the good news. He was surprised that Kingston had fixed it that fast. It had taken less than twenty minutes. Kingston told Leland the ice should be good by the time the kids started arriving, but Leland should have the owner check things over still.

Leland thanked him and handed Kingston a black leather binder. We left him in his office and went to sit on the stands.

"What's that?" I asked, pointing to the binder.

"It's the Coach's drills and notes about the team. We need to see what they're working on and struggling with so we can build a good lesson for them this morning. We've only got a couple hours before the kids show up."

I gawked down at him as his words registered. "A couple *hours*? We got here two and a half hours early?"

Kingston nodded while studying the binders. "I wanted to bring you early so we could go over the plan for practice. Good thing too, since we had to flip the rink breakers."

Okay. But two hours early was still excessive just to go over a lesson plan for kids. At least, that's what I thought. Apparently, Kingston took this quite seriously. Something he proved further when he whipped out a notebook from his bag and flipped it open to show a hand-drawn schedule.

"Okay, so we're going to start with an introduction from the kids. I cycle around the city

78

mostly, so I haven't met this group of kids yet. Then I'll let you lead the stretching."

He was dedicated. Or maybe it was called being a control freak. I was just as dedicated to my charity back in Seattle, and I always made sure the kids had a fun and educational time, but this man was taking it to a whole other level.

He went on for a while, referring to Coach Leland's notes and outlining every minute of the schedule. I paid as much attention as I could, although I admittedly zoned out a couple times. By the time he was done, we had about forty-five minutes left before practice and the zamboni was ready to come out.

While it was doing its route around the ice, Kingston and I got geared up. Once we were dressed and the zamboni was done, we got onto the fresh ice, Kingston hauling the last bag with him. I took a few laps in full gear around the rink, warming up a little and enjoying the crisp air coming up off the surface of the ice.

As I was doing my lap, Coach Leland and the ice rink owner, who had shown up mid-way through outlining our lesson plan, brought the nets onto the ice and stuck them into their places. As Kingston had a quick chat with them, I went up to one of the goals and dropped my mask, stick, gloves, and water bottle on the top. By the time I joined Kingston at the other side of the ice, the coach and owner were gone.

I helped him take out some of the equipment and set up multiple lines of tiny cones.

According to Leland's notes, the kids were working on improving their stickhandling. I doubted I could do much to help them improve on that, but Kingston had some of the best hands in the league. We set the cones up on half of the ice, leaving the other half clear.

With time to kill before the kiddos were supposed to show up, we skated around slowly, loosening up our legs.

"Want to race?" Kingston asked, pointing at the lines of tiny orange cones.

I perked up in interest. "Hell yeah! Give me your extra stick." He went and grabbed it from the bench outside. My goalie stick would have been too clunky to do this well. Not that I expected to win. I wasn't that crazy. But I *was* a professional athlete; I would never turn down a challenge.

Kingston dumped out a bucket of pucks and we both took one. Then I lined up at one of the lines, Kingston taking the neighboring one.

I counted us down—ready and go! We wove the pucks between the cones, going as fast as possible while also trying not to knock them over. Halfway through my line, I stopped hearing the cuts of Kingston's blade against the ice, but I refused to look up and continued, focusing on my puck. And ... done!

Kingston was leaning against his stick, smiling down at me. Cocky bastard. We looked at our lines. A half-dozen of my cones were knocked over, more than that moved out of their original places. Kingston's line? Kingston's line was fucking flawless.

A hummed rendition of "We Are the Champions" reached my ears, and I whipped around in faux outrage. I slid up to him and boxed his shoulder. If I were a two-hundred-pound defenseman during a game, Kingston would have dropped his glove and gone at me. Now, he just raised his hands in surrender as my shoving sent him gliding backward on his skates.

"Oh, it is on, Your Majesty," I said then went to the net and retrieved my glove and blocker. I held them out to him and taunted, "Whatchu got?"

He chuckled deeply and skated up to me. "Okay, Warren. Let's do it." He put on the glove and blocker and grabbed my stick but forwent the mask—it was too small for him.

I grabbed some pucks from center ice and got into position.

"You ready?" I asked, smiling across the ice at him.

"Just don't break my face, Warren. It's all I've got going for me." He matched my grin and pushed back and forth off his skates, getting ready for me. His form was God-awful.

I skated up to him at a moderate speed, my leg pads bogging down my movements. I didn't bother with fancy tricks, knowing the puck would fly off to the side if I tried.

I deked to the left, and he lunged. I slipped it through his five-hole, taking advantage of his lack of pads. I sang my own version of "We Are the

Champions" as I circled around the net. I turned to skate backward toward the pile of pucks as Kingston whirled around, his face incredulous.

I winked at him. *Not so easy now, was it?*

He squinted his eyes at me, a smile twitching the scar on his lips, and settled back into position. He jerked the stick at me, his message clear. Bring it.

We played around until the kids showed up.

6

"Could you believe that Xavier kid?" I asked Kingston and flung my bag into the back of his truck with a grunt. Hosting a practice while trying to wrangle a bunch of children was just as brutal as any practice in the NHL. Pee-wee coaches deserved a raise.

Most of the kids in the program were already pretty good, but Xavier, at just twelve years old, was miles ahead of everyone else. Unfortunately, he knew it. I had never seen a kid so damn sure of himself and so … completely unliked. The team must have been together for a while because no one was surprised by Xavier's brashness, but I had to give the kid props, he knew when to shut up and listen to his superiors. That might be his saving grace.

Kingston heaved his bags in. "He could go pro one day. If his mouth doesn't get him into trouble before then."

I chuckled. "He reminds me of me."

"Oh? So, you were always a smart ass?"

"Since the day I was born." I was a menace, but I was usually able to back up my cockiness.

We hopped into the car, and Kingston drove us out of the rink's parking lot.

"Please tell me you're as hungry as I am," Kingston said.

Oh, thank you. "Hell, yes."

"Good. I don't think my stomach would have survived dropping you off before I got something to eat. Are you in the mood for anything in particular?"

I looked around in thought at the vaguely familiar area then pointed to the stoplight a few yards ahead. "Take a left."

Kingston shrugged and followed my directions until we pulled up to a small diner ten minutes later.

"The Green UFO," he read the sign as we hopped out of the truck.

"Oh yeah. This place is awesome. You'll love it."

"Okay, if you say so."

Kingston held the door open for me and the smell of burgers and fries wafted to me. The diner was just like I remembered it—hella cheesy. The place had been around since the 50s and looked like a restaurant out of time. Except, instead of the classic red and white color scheme of most retro diners, this was green and white ... and covered in alien memorabilia.

"Wow," Kingston muttered under his breath, looking around at the tacky decor.

"I know," I whispered back with an uncontrollable smile on my face.

A smiling hostess welcomed us with Spock's famous hand gesture, plastic antennae bobbing atop her head. "Greetings. Just two?" At our nods, she pushed away from the podium and led us to our table on sparkly green roller skates. She set down our menus, informed us our server would be here soon, and rolled away.

Kingston shrugged out of his leather jacket, and we sat down in the green vinyl booth. He relaxed into the seat, and I followed suit. Since our little competition, and the practice with the kids, Kingston had started to chill out around me. He was opening up, and I was actually starting to think this might work.

"This place is amazing. How'd you know about it? I thought you were a spoiled little rich kid that never left Manhattan."

I flipped him off, but a smile was pulling at my lips. He had a point. "I *was* a spoiled little rich kid. Until I met Mason. He used to live around here. Our pee-wee team practiced at a rink a few miles away."

"The one we were just at?" Kingston asked with a raised eyebrow.

"No, no. One in the opposite direction."

We quieted as a woman dressed like an alien waitress skated up to us. We quickly ordered our drinks—both of us choosing water—and the waitress glided away to give us time to look over the menu.

"Wait," Kingston said suddenly. "What were you doing on Frey's team? Pee-wee teams are divided by area."

I fought the urge to fiddle with the alien-green vinyl under my thigh. "They usually are, but after I met Mason and we became friends, I switched over to his team as soon as I could."

"And your parents just let you?"

"Uh ... yeah. They were just glad I made a friend. I was only really interested in hockey, and it wasn't like the kids on my team were thrilled about a girl being with them," I said shyly. Damn, I sounded like a loser. To be honest, it hadn't been that bad; I was—and still am—more focused on blocking pucks than making friends. So, when I noticed the boys not responding to my attempts at making friends, I dropped it. But my parents were getting worried that my only friends were the goal posts, so when I met Mason, they did everything in their power to support me. Just like they did with everything in my life.

Kingston winced, and I cocked my head at the sudden mood shift, waiting for the question he obviously wanted to ask. Eventually, he got it out. "I know you said you weren't before, but are you sure you're not mad at us, Warren? About the game, I mean."

I sighed and was granted a moment to think as our waitress came back, dropped off our waters, and took our orders. Kingston wanted a burger, and I decided on a chicken wrap. I waited for the waitress to skate away again before I answered.

"No. I was never really mad at you guys to begin with. A little irritated at the situation, maybe, but if I were to be mad at anyone, it would be Hansson. It was his call; you guys were just following orders. It's not that big of a deal. I'm kind of used to it."

Kingston sighed. "Yeah. That's kind of the problem. You shouldn't be used to it."

I pursed my lips. "Objectively, I know that, but it's almost second nature at this point. I've never had a team that fully supported me. The only player who's ever had my back is Mason. I've learned to adapt," I said, then smiled ruefully. "I guess that's why I 'don't play well with others' as Coach said."

Kingston didn't respond right away, and I could practically see the wheels turning in his head. Suddenly, he jolted straight in his booth and nodded with determination. "Okay then. I'll be your friend."

"But ... you're already my mentor. Doesn't that force you to be my friend anyway?"

Kingston grimaced and waved his hand as if batting away my comment. "I've never really been a great mentor. I mean, I give good advice for hockey things, but when it comes to life problems... Let's just say there's a reason I'm not the captain."

I sipped my water in contemplation. Was that the reason Kingston turned down the captain role? I always figured he declined the position because he was too busy or because he just didn't like being a teacher. "But you want to help me deal with my life problems? Is this because you feel guilty? Because I don't need your pity."

"No," he denied emphatically. "I don't pity you at all. I saw you on that ice. You're damn strong. You basically played the first part of that game by yourself, but you shouldn't have had to. So, I'm going to make sure you're never left hanging like that again."

"By being my friend?"

"Yes. By being your friend," he said then raised an eyebrow, awaiting my answer.

I stared at his eyebrow absentmindedly from across the table. *How did he do that?* I could never move just one eyebrow, and I'd tried. It was no wonder Kingston could do it though; the man could do everything. So, if he said he could help me, I had to believe him.

Fighting back the part of me that balked at the implication that I needed help, I cleared my throat. "Ok. So, what do you want to talk about, friend?"

"I don't know. What do friends usually talk about?"

"Aside from hockey? Relationships, maybe? What about that girl you're dating? What was her name again?"

"Sarah."

"Right, Sarah. How is she?"

"I don't know. We broke up." The voice could have come from a robot with how much emotion it held.

I searched Kingston's face, trying to see if he was hiding sadness behind his indifference. I caught the slightest hint of regret in his eyes, but he seemed mostly fine.

"Oh. That sucks. I'm sorry," I said, not knowing what else to do in this situation.

He shrugged and took a sip from his water as silence stretched, long but not entirely awkward.

His scar danced around his cup, and my mouth moved before I could stop it. "Was that from a puck?"

"Huh?" he mumbled, looking up at me through his lashes.

Going with my slip of the tongue, I forged ahead and pointed at the scar on his lip that carved a prominent line through his dark stubble. "That scar. Is it from a puck?"

He reached up and traced it instinctually, his blunt fingernails scratching against his stubble with a light rasping noise. "Yeah. I got it when I was ... fourteen maybe. Me and my friends were messing around on an outdoor rink, without any helmets, and a puck came up out of nowhere and got me."

"Did it break any teeth?" While, with better gear and dental procedures, missing teeth were not as rampant in hockey as they used to be, holes in players' smiles weren't uncommon.

"Nope," Kingston said with a pop at the end of the word. Next thing I knew, I was looking at perfect rows of pearly white teeth coming from the most breath-taking smile I had ever seen.

The corners of his lips were sharper than a skate blade. Crinkles appeared at the corner of his eyes, bringing his stoic grey eyes to life. If it weren't for the scar on his lip or his slightly crooked nose, he would be as perfect as a Greek statue. "Didn't break or chip anything. Although I was bleeding like a stuck pig."

I huffed out a small laugh, thankful when he put his smile back in his pocket. I had only seen hints of tiny grins from him and the fake, tight-lipped smiles that he gave to the press. Even with the kiddos earlier, he only broke out soft looks, nothing like the giant smile that was currently blinding me. I could only be glad he never revealed it during a game. I would freeze in place if I ever saw it on the ice. "I could imagine. Maybe you should wear a cage."

Kingston cracked another smile, this one just a twitch of his lips. "Aw, c'mon, I was a kid. And can you really judge? Unlike the rest of us, you get to wear a full-face mask all the time."

I pursed my lips for a moment, deciding if I wanted to admit to my childhood stupidity, then gave in, in the name of our newfound friendship. "Okay, fine. I'm going to show you something, but you can't tell anyone else. Ever!"

Kingston leaned forward, his elbows on the table, and eagerly searched my face. "I promise."

I took a deep breath then tilted my head back, showing him the underside of my chin.

A moment passed in silence then I felt something touch my neck. I froze as his fingertip grazed the scar under my chin. "Wait. That little scar? I can barely see it. Why are you embarrassed?"

Kingston took his finger away, and I lowered my chin, trying to remember what he just said. Oh, yeah. I took a sip of my water to relieve my suddenly dry throat then answered Kingston.

"It's not the scar so much as the story behind it that's embarrassing. It was my third game in juniors. Like always, I was trying to prove myself to the guys." I paused and snorted, smiling ruefully as my face heated. No doubt my face would be tomato red in a minute—the downside of pasty, Russian skin. "We were warming up before the game, and I was blocking shots when one of the guys' girlfriends came to the glass to say hi to him. She was *really* pretty..."

Kingston chuckled as I trailed off, knowing where this was going. "Please tell me you didn't get distracted by a girl, Warren. Please."

I laughed in pain and winced at the memory. "I didn't even notice that I took off my mask as I was staring at her until I was flat on the ice and all I could see was the ceiling of the arena."

With a half-groan, half-laugh, Kingston slapped his hand over his face. Then he took it away to give me a faux-disappointed look. "What is it kids these days say? Something about hopeless lesbians?"

I snorted. "You mean 'useless lesbian.' And at least I'm not as bad anymore. Also, really? 'Kids these days?' Your age is showing," I taunted. Admittedly, he was only thirty, but I had just turned twenty-one. Add in the short lifespan of professional athletes, and the guy was getting up there in years. Still, I would bet he had at least four more seasons in him.

The waitress returned with our food, and all conversation stopped as we dug in like starving wolves.

Ten minutes later, Kingston finished off his burger and leaned back into the booth, gazing at me from under food-lazy eyelids. "You're paying, right?"

"The superstar is cheap? I should have guessed."

"Hey, I'm at the end of my contract. I could be out of a job in a couple months."

Yeah, and I'm the best sniper in the league. I managed to hold in my eye roll. No doubt management will be bumping into the salary cap when they sign Kingston on for a few more years. And they will be happy to do so; he was worth it.

Still, I acquiesced. "I'll pay on one condition."

Kingston arched a brow. *How the hell...?*

"You have to order a dessert with me. I can't break my diet alone."

"So, you're bringing me down with you?" Sebastian asked with an amused smirk.

"Sure am. Do we have a deal?"

"Deal."

"Great. Let's go," I said as I popped out of the booth. I threw down four twenties on the table and gestured for Kingston to follow me.

He slowly slid out of his side of the booth, grabbing his jacket as he stood. "Wait. Where are we going? I assumed you meant a desert here."

"Nope. I've got somewhere even better than here in mind."

Forty seconds later, Kingston and I slid into a store a couple doors down from The Green UFO.

As the doors closed behind us, I took a deep inhale, breathing in the scents of sugar and my childhood. I felt like I had just come back from pee-wee practice with Mason, sweating and craving something sweet.

The store was painted with shades of pink, yellow, and blue, making it feel as if you were standing inside of a cake. The white chairs looked like they were made from buttercream frosting, and the tables were giant macaroons. It being too late for the lunch crowd, no one was sitting. Besides us, only one other person was in the store, being rung up at the counter.

"Wow, look at that menu," Kingston breathed out, eyes on the big board covering the entire back wall.

I smiled and searched it to see if anything new had been added. The large chalkboard held over two-hundred items, ranging from over-the-top cakes and pies to specialty ice cream and s'mores. But despite the already huge selection, there was always something new. *Cool. They added alcoholic ice cream! I'll have to come back for that sometime.*

When we got to the display case, Kingston ordered a simple sweet cream cone with chocolate sauce.

I picked something that, for all the times I'd ordered it, had never been written down on the menu. "Could I get a large vanilla milkshake? And, if you have any, could you throw a Twix bar into the blender? They're my favorite."

"Sure," the cashier said. "Let me check in the back really quick."

While she pushed through the swinging gate behind her, I took out my phone, took a quick picture of the menu, and sent it to Drew and Mason. They would be so jealous. Next, I started typing a message on a different text chain, but before I could finish the sentence, a shout from the back of the shop drew my head up.

"What? A Twix milkshake?" an excited voice exclaimed.

Suddenly, the gate swung open with enough force to bang into the wall, and a sphere was speeding toward my face. I whipped up my hand, and the object hit my palm with a hard *thwack.* Instead of the usual tennis ball, my hand held … an orange? I stared at it in confusion for a second then met the eyes of my assailant.

The thrower marched around the counter with purpose, and I moved to meet her.

"An orange?" I asked.

"I didn't have any tennis balls handy," the woman said and pulled me into a bone-crushing hug. She may not look it with her slight stature, but years of kneading bread and mixing batter had made her arms into solid muscle. "Riley Alina Warren. Why didn't you tell me you were in the area?"

"Sorry, Ms. Frey," I said into the hair tickling the bottom of my nose. "Kingston and I were just doing an event and decided to get some lunch. Now we're here for processed sugar."

"Frey?" Kingston asked.

Ms. Frey let go of me, and we turned to Kingston. I'd forgotten he was there for a second.

"Sorry. Kingston, this is Madeline Frey, Mason's mom. Ms. Frey, this is—"

"I know who he is," Ms. Frey cut me off. "It's nice to meet you, Sebastian."

"You too."

They shook hands, and I stifled a giggle. Kingston's hulking figure made Ms. Frey even smaller and cuter. The same green eyes, beachy hair, and tan skin that made Mason the spitting image of a surfer dude made his mother look like a fairy.

"Mason has told me a lot about you, about all of you," Ms. Frey said conversationally, then narrowed her eyes.

Oh, no.

Her frilly apron shook as she put her hands on her hips and glared up at Kingston. "You know, he was ready to hunt you and Jones down after that stunt you pulled. Now, I don't usually condone that sort of behavior, but if you ever do that again, rest assured, the last thing you'll remember before waking up in the hospital is the business end of your own hockey stick rearranging your face. And it won't be Mason holding it, it will be me."

Kingston's jaw had dropped halfway through her speech, and his eyebrows now seemed to live in his hairline. His gaping mouth flapped open and close, but before he could sputter out a reply, a bell dinged, echoing around the silent shop.

"Sweet cream cone with chocolate drizzle and a Twix milkshake." The cashier put our orders on the counter.

I stared at them in confusion. Neither Kingston nor I had paid, too distracted by Ms. Frey.

"Thank you, Nicole," Ms. Frey said then turned to me. "Don't think you will get away with paying in here, missy. They're on the house, of course."

I smiled. "Thank you, Ms. Frey."

"Yes. Thank you, Ms. Frey," Kingston echoed. It looked like his mouth was finally working.

She jabbed two fingers at her eyes then thrust them toward Kingston in the international sign of "I'm watching you" as she headed back around the counter and into the back.

"Well, she's terrifying," Kingston said then paused. "Why isn't Mason like that on the ice?"

I snorted and went up to the counter to collect our treats. "Because Mason is a puppy."

I took my milkshake, and Kingston plucked his cone from its little holder.

Kingston took an experimental taste of his cone, and his eyes lit up. "Damn. That's amazing."

"Worth the calories?"

"Definitely."

We took a seat at a purple macaroon to avoid going out into the February chill. However, despite the cold weather, the ice cream hit the spot.

"Why did she throw an orange at you?" Kingston asked suddenly.

I stared at him in confusion for a second before I understood. "Oh. Well, she usually throws tennis balls. It's a game I started playing as a kid. I was training my hand-eye coordination with some tennis balls, but I was getting bored. So, I asked my brother to chuck some at me, but the little asshole didn't stop after I was done. He kept on pelting me with them out of the blue. Sometimes he would wait weeks to give me a false sense of security before he attacked. Eventually, Mason and my family got into it—although my parents didn't throw as hard as the boys. I had to keep my head on a permeant swivel. I still do. Sometimes I feel like a Navy SEAL, checking every room I walk into for flying projectiles, but it's fun and one of the reasons my reaction time is so quick."

"Have you ever gotten hit in the face?"

My face heated slightly. "Oh, yeah. More than a few times."

He chuckled and ate more of his ice cream. I sucked on my milkshake to hide my smile.

Most people would look like a little kid when licking an ice cream cone, getting food around their mouth and on the tip of their nose. But Kingston, with all his self-control, on and off the ice, ate with military-like precision. Not an ounce of ice cream landed on his face or dripped onto his hand. Still, as his pink tongue flicked out to get more of the sweet cream, I couldn't help but think it was cute.

If she were here, my mom would pinch his cheeks and call him a little *gospodin*. I'd seen her do it to Mason and Drew enough times when they acted like little gentlemen. She had always appreciated good manners.

She would probably try to set me up with him, I thought randomly, then immediately froze in horror at the fluttering in my stomach. Shit. I knew that feeling.

Chill out, chill out, chill out.

I exhaled slowly, keeping my feelings from spreading onto my face for Kingston to see. I took another breath in and released it.

This was no big deal. I was an adult, and I could deal with this. I knew I was attracted to him, but I'd already decided last night to ignore it. So what if it wasn't just physical like I'd thought and I actually liked him as a person? It didn't change anything; nothing could happen. We were teammates and friends, nothing more.

Air flooded my lungs with a stutter as I struggled to keep my composure.
Fuck.

7

"**D**o you think women can do everything men can do?"

Okay, I was done with this shit. I slid out of the small swarm of reporters that had been hounding me with questions for the last five minutes and shouldered my duffle. I had three hours before the team got on the plane, and I hadn't packed anything. I didn't have time to waste answering bullshit questions.

I was about to go on my first road trip with the Blizzards and had just been leaving the arena after an early morning team meeting when Garza, a rookie forward, asked me to block some of his shots. Since I was trying to make more friends on the team, I couldn't say no.

After working with Garza, just when I thought I was free to run to my house, I was surrounded in the hallways by these guys. There wasn't as much press as usual, as we weren't playing a game here today and it was only eight in the morning. Their questions went off the rails quickly though.

With some quick and sneaky footwork, I escaped the reporters and the arena. I headed home with a plan to take a shower, throw a bunch of crap into a bag, and hitch a ride with Mason to the charter plane. Thankfully, when I pulled up to my house, Mason's car was already parked outside. He was undoubtedly playing on my Xbox and eating all the food in my fridge again.

But when I went inside, I didn't see him in the living room, although his luggage was packed by the front door.

"Mason?" I called out. No answer. Huh. Might be in the bathroom.

I dropped my stuff on the floor to sort out later and headed up to my room. I kicked open my door, already taking off my hoodie, needing to get in high gear if I didn't want to be late. The fabric blinded me for a second, and when I pulled it over my eyes, I saw a man staring at me from the edge of my bed.

"Jesus!" I chucked my hoodie at Mason for scaring the crap out of me and headed for my bathroom, walking off the startlement. "What the hell, man?"

Mason got up and followed me. "Sorry."

I turned on the shower and faced him, concerned. He sounded somber; he looked it too, leaning against the sink, his arms folded and his head down.

"Oh my God." I grabbed him by the arms, and he looked up. "Is your mom okay?" I had just seen her yesterday with Kingston and she looked fine then.

"She's fine," he reassured me, but bit his lip, looking away from me

I breathed a sigh. "Then what's up? I'm pretty sure your dog didn't die. You don't have one," I said, trying to lighten the mood.

"I don't want you to be mad."

Mad? I studied him. He was starting to worry me. I could count on one hand how many times I'd gotten truly pissed at Mason and still have three fingers left. I nodded for him to get on with it.

"I'm going to go on a date with Drew."

I took a second to process.

Then I screamed and launched myself at him. I squeezed him to me and squealed into his ear. I might have shaken him, or I could have just been vibrating with joy—I couldn't tell. When I finally pulled back and saw his wincing face, I loosed my grip a little but didn't let go. "Fucking finally!" I shouted to the heavens.

"You're not mad?" Mason asked, looking as timid as I had ever seen him.

"Of course, I'm not mad, you fucking idiot!" I definitely shook him this time. "I've been waiting for this day for years, Mase!"

Oh my God! This was finally happening. I wanted to dance around the room with him in celebration, but we needed to get going.

"Crap. I have to shower. Don't move," I said, got undressed, and hopped under the shower spray as Mason sat on the closed toilet lid. His silhouette was blurry through the frosted glass door.

"Tell me everything," I shouted over the running water as I lathered up my hair.

"Well, I was going to go home a little bit after you left with Kingston yesterday, but Drew came home early from his meeting. He had a bunch of groceries and started making *blini*. So of course, I stayed."

Ah. *Blini* were essentially Russian crepes and one of the only things I could make consistently well. I'd bribed Mason with them a million times; they were his weakness. Add in the fact that Drew was cooking, and Mason wouldn't have left this house if his life depended on it.

"We got to talking, and somehow, we ended up on the couch. Then we were kissing." His voice turned shy at the end until I could just barely hear him over the water.

I rinsed my hair then applied conditioner, rubbing harshly with my excitement. "Who kissed who first?" I asked like a teenage girl. I couldn't help it; it was finally happening!

"I don't really know. We kinda just fell into each other."

I was mid "awe" when a horrible thought occurred to me. "Please tell me you guys didn't have sex on that couch!"

I could practically feel Mason rolling his eyes. "No. We decided to go slowly and make a real relationship out of this. We don't want to mess things up."

They could never mess things up. If there were ever any two people that were made for each other, it was Drew and Mason. They weren't the best of friends when Mason and I were kids; Drew was too old and cool for us, but Mason had been in love with him forever. I've had to watch him moon over Drew since Mason met him.

When our parents died, and Drew transferred to New York to raise me, he got to know Mason more as an almost-adult. It took longer for Drew than it did for Mason, but eventually, Drew had fallen just as hard. Of course, he didn't act on it. Mason was seventeen and had a promising career in a homophobic field. Drew, my sweet, overprotective, mother-hen brother, didn't want Mason to jeopardize his life for Drew. He left the city without a word about his feelings when Mason and I were drafted.

I never knew if the guys had ever realized that their feelings were mutual. I had to physically silence myself on more than one occasion, having promised both of them not to reveal their secrets to the other. It was painful to watch sometimes, but I had faith that it would work itself out in the end. And it looked like my patience was paying off. This was the start of the rest of their lives.

I finished showering, wrapped myself in a towel, and stepped out.

Still sitting on the toilet lid, Mason had a small smile on his face, his eyes off in the distance. Ah, they were so cute!

"Hey," I said softly. His eyes focused on me then widened at my serious expression. "I truly wish the best for you two, and I want you to know that no matter what happens between you guys, you will always be family. If you happen to become my brother in the future, that'll just be icing on the cake."

Mason shot up, and the next thing I knew, I was being crushed in a hug. I chuckled and wrapped an arm around him, keeping a hold on my towel with the other.

I took the seat beside Mason as everyone got settled onto the plane. He had the window seat and was already putting his noise-canceling headphones on. It was the only reprieve he had from me. I had been bugging him about Drew for the last couple hours, but I recognized my annoyingness and let Mason get some rest for tonight's game. As per usual, he was unconscious in two minutes flat. I took a picture of him and sent it off to Drew.

He responded immediately with a picture of him in a fancy office with the city skyline behind him. Then a text came, telling me that he loved me. I told him I loved him too. It had become a habit for us whenever we got on or off planes.

Twenty minutes later, I sat stiff-backed in my seat as the plane taxied down the runway and took off. Once we were in the air, I unclenched my hands from where I hadn't realized they dug into the armrests. It had been almost six years since the plane crash that killed my parents, but I still wasn't comfortable on planes; I didn't think I ever would be. Drew had it easier, but I could never fully shake my nerves. Still, I was getting better.

It only took a few rounds of breathing exercises, and by the time the seatbelt light turned off, I was as calm as I could be in the situation. I undid my buckle and reached for my backpack to pull out my iPad and review tapes of Vancouver's shooters for the dozenth time.

But before I could unzip the bag, a sharp whistle came from the back of the plane then, "Warren, heads up!"

I whipped around then immediately shot out of my seat to catch the tennis ball flying down the aisle. I caught it with a solid *thunk* and stared incredulously at the person who had thrown it.

Kingston waved me over as he sat back down in the seat he had vacated to launch a ball at me. Confused, I hiked my backpack over my shoulder and walked over, swaying slightly with the movements of the plane. On either side of the aisle, most of the team were in their own worlds, either asleep or watching videos on their phones.

"Nice catch," Kingston said when I got closer. Behind him, Ethan Jones had an impressed face on.

"Eh. It's not like it was a hard throw," I chirped with a smile and tossed the ball back to Kingston. As it landed in his hand, I noticed for the first time how bright yellow it was. Had Kingston bought fresh tennis balls just to throw them at me? The thought sparked a feeling that I pushed down quickly. He was just trying to be my friend. Because we were friends. Just friends. "What's going on here?"

"Texas hold 'em," Jones said, organizing colorful chips on his tray table. "You ever play?"

The "poker table" consisted of four aisle seats forming a square. Jones and Erik "Ice" Berg, the teammate who had laughed at my Russian chirp to Lukin, sat in the back two seats. They both had teammates passed out next to them, headphones on. Kingston sat in an empty row in front of Jones, leaving the row across the aisle from him open. This must be his first attempt to help me make friends on the team. I sat, dropped my backpack onto the free window seat, and angled my body so I could see Berg behind me and Jones diagonally across from me. Copying the boys, I lowered my tray table.

"Yes, I have played," I said with all the confidence of a professional competitor. Little did they know that I, Riley Alina Warren, was the world's *worst* poker player. Drew had taught me a long time ago, and while I got the rules, I was a stubborn bastard. I couldn't force myself to fold, not even when I really should. What was my strength on the ice—my inability to give up—was my downfall at poker. My strategy was to win as much as I could before they realized that I wasn't bluffing, I was just horrible.

Kingston broke out a deck of cards and shuffled with the dexterity of a professional magician, the cards moving fluidly between his big hands.

"Oh-ho-ho," Berg laughed, his blond beard shaking with his rumbling chest. Berg was an intimidating Nordic man, and his beard was just as large as the rest of him. "Well then, Warren. It's a two-hundred-dollar buy-in. Think you can swing it?"

"I think my wallet can take it," I teased, pulled said wallet out of my backpack, and dropped the cash into the kitty piled on Kingston's tray table, already saying goodbye to it. I knew I wasn't going to win it back, but damned if I wouldn't try.

Berg and I put our blind bids on the edges of our tray tables, and the game was on. Kingston dealt out the cards. I came up with two eights and leaned back in my seat, a confident smile on my face. This was a good start. Let them think I was always this cocky.

As we settled into the game, small talk filled the space between bets.

"Is your wife pissed at you, Berg?" Jones asked.

"A little."

"You're married?" I asked Berg. I hadn't known that. But to be fair, I didn't know much about the guy other than he was Swedish, a damn good defenseman, and understood some Russian.

Kingston put down the flop, and I tried my best to keep the smile off my face. I didn't succeed.

"Yeah, eight years today."

I winced. "Ouch. Missing your anniversary?"

"Yeah, but that's the life, you know," he said with a shrug. Everyone nodded.

"And you chose to get married in the middle of the season," Jones added.

"At least he *has* a girl," Kingston playfully shot at Jones. I couldn't hold back my snort. Damn.

"Hey, you could have said that a week ago, but not now."

Kingston grimaced slightly, and I wondered if was just being blasé about his breakup when I asked yesterday.

"If it makes you feel better, I don't have a girlfriend either," I confessed and called Kingston's raise.

Kingston's grimace didn't let up at my comment. If anything, it got worse.

"But you have time to find a girl, Warren. We're getting old, and our pretty faces won't last forever," Jones said.

"Hey, at least we have the game," I said and raised an imaginary drink in salute, avoiding Kingston's eyes. Despite what Jones and everybody outside of my family believed, I didn't always want a girl. In fact, I could practically feel the needle on my Kinsey scale shifting, and it was all thanks to a man that I couldn't have.

"Here, here," Jones cheered and copied my toast with a water bottle.

Berg smiled through his thick beard, and Kingston just shrugged his eyebrows.

A couple moments later, I won the first round and gloated with faux confidence. It wouldn't last.

I was proven correct as we played a few more rounds. I lost every one and was the first out. I pouted at their teasing and pulled my legs up onto my seat to watch the rest of the game.

"So, you ready for tonight, Warren?" Jones asked, folding at Berg's raise.

I peeked around my seat to get a look at Berg's cards. He angled them forward to let me see his hand. It was garbage.

"I'm always ready. That is if you guys are going to help me out this time." I poked Berg in the shoulder and shot him a smile to let them know that I had no hard feelings. The guys had been perfectly professional since then. That didn't mean I wasn't going to give them hell about it though.

Jones looked at his feet, and Berg smiled back at me shyly. Kingston just smirked, the scar on his lips twitching teasingly. He knew I was just busting their balls.

"I think you can handle yourself no matter what we do, Warren," Kingston said. He folded his hand, and Berg collected his winnings.

Wow. To get a compliment like that from a player as good as Kingston was enough to shoot my self-esteem to the moon. He must have noticed my surprise because his smirk turned into that breath-taking smile, and I was grinning back before I could catch myself.

"Damn right, she can," Jones seconded, jerking my attention away from Kingston. Berg nodded in agreement.

"Thanks, guys," I said then instinctually deflected by being a chirpy bastard. "But I don't want to steal all your thunder. It's rude to take from the elderly."

They all laughed, and Berg handed me half of his chips, putting me back in the game. Awesome.

The next round began, and I made sure to keep my eyes on my cards and off a certain assistant captain. We played until Berg finished wiping the floor with us and bullshitted until the plane touched down in Vancouver.

It wasn't until after the team dropped our stuff off in the hotel we were staying at and then headed out for a late lunch to fuel up for the game that I realized I went the whole flight and landing without any anxiety about the plane crashing.

8

I deflected the last puck with my stick and slapped my glove down on it before it could rebound anywhere. A groan came from the crowd, but I smiled and whooped in victory.

Seconds later, my team swarmed me, giving me hugs and slaps in excitement as the game ended. We eventually broke up and lined up for handshakes with the other team. As Kingston skated by to join the end of the line, he reached out with his stick and slashed me on the pads. At my questioning look, he gave me an approving nod, and my face heated.

We shook hands with our opponents, and I got more smiles than I thought I would. If any team was already used to women in the league, it was this one. I made sure to give friendly handshakes to everyone, but when I got to the end of the line, instead of a hand reaching for me, I got pulled into an embrace cushioned by layers of pads.

"Nice game, kid," Rachel McCarthy said into my ear, her voice barely audible over the noise in the arena. She might have only been a year older than me, but she was my idol—the first woman to join the NHL. I'd always expected to be the first, the woman to break that glass ceiling in the league, but when she was drafted a year before me, I couldn't have been happier to have my expectations shattered. She took off a lot of pressure from me and handled the responsibility of being the first way better than I would have.

I almost tripped over my feet when I met her during my time with the Blades, and she was just as excited to meet the other woman in the league as I was, even if we didn't play together. It was surreal, and today, finally, two women were on the ice, playing against each other in the NHL. Times were changing.

I kind of wanted to punch her.

It would have probably been the only time I ever got into a fight during a game. The regular boys aren't too keen on fighting ladies, so I've never been in a fight on the ice. I felt like I was missing out. Maybe next time we played against each other, Rachel and I could drop gloves. Just to get the whole hockey experience.

Later, I followed my team into the locker room and collapsed into my locker, not having the energy to start undressing yet. The game was close, but I shut Vancouver down during the shootout. My thighs were burning, my ribs were stinging where I took a puck to the side, and sweat was dripping down my face. Still, I couldn't stop smiling. I had dominated my first NHL shootout!

I got a few more kudos from the guys as we settled down to wait for Coach. Beside me, Lukin was seething. Dude needed to chill. He got to play tomorrow, and if he spent more time practicing instead of hating me, he might already be the permanent goalie.

As it was, the team hadn't made a decision yet. The season was coming to an end soon and there was no way we were going to the playoffs, not after Hall and Stanton, the Blizzards' other goalies, were injured at the beginning of the season. So Coach and management have been trying out new plays and switching between Lukin and me as goalie to see who fit the best. There was no guarantee that either of us were going to stay after this season, but it was rumored that Hall might be out for good. When Stanton comes back, the Blizzards will be in need of another goalie. So, as far as Lukin and I were concerned, the competition was on.

After everyone fell quiet, Coach gave a quick overview, knowing we were all ready to wash off. It was a tough game, and everybody was sweating through their gear. Most guys already had their sweaters thrown in their lockers and were slowly stripping their gear off. I was right there with them, stripping off my top layers too.

The second Coach finished talking, half the guys streamed into the showers. I went to the women's showers and enjoyed the hot water.

I took my time washing up, and by the time I returned to the locker room, wrapped in a towel, most of the guys were already dressed.

I quickly went to my locker and pulled the curtain surrounding my area closed. It was a struggle to pull on my panties and bra while scrubbing my hair dry with my towel, but I managed. Decent enough in my sports bra and boy short panties, I yanked the curtain open and immediately jumped back from the big body crowding my space.

"Jesus, man," I breathed out and shoved Kingston lightly for scaring me. My hand stuck to his shower-wet clavicle for a second before I pulled it away. He was only in his slacks, his tattooed torso and arms left bare. I kept my eyes firmly on his and not any lower. *We're in the fucking locker room with the whole team*, I reminded myself harshly, not wanting a repeat of the other day. *And he's just your friend!*

His scar twitched. "Damn, Warren. Where are those reflexes from thirty minutes ago?" Kingston chirped, his voice low and rough. After the roaring of the crowds, his voice was like balm to my ears.

No!

I cleared my throat and wiped the corner of my eye with my middle finger, pointedly keeping eye contact with the distracting man.

Kingston smirked again but stopped teasing me. "You want to hang with us tonight?"

"Depends. What are we doing?"

"Well, we can't go out. We have a curfew, and I stopped showing up hungover to games twelve years ago."

"You got drafted twelve years ago," I pointed out.

"I only went through that pain once, Warren, but it was enough." He shuddered in exaggeration, and I chuckled. "Jones and I are just going to hang out at the hotel bar. We each get one beer tonight, and we want to make it last. Frey's invited too."

"Okay, I'm down."

"Cool, but you might want to wear a little more than that." He gestured to my half-undressed self.

I almost snorted. It wasn't like he hadn't seen me in less. Still, I turned to my locker, bent down to put on my slacks, then turned back around. "Better?" I asked Kingston, who was still standing there, his back rod-straight.

He looked at something over his shoulder and coughed into his hand. "Yeah," he said to me, his voice even rougher than before, and walked back to his locker abruptly.

I shrugged off his weirdness and finished dressing.

I showed up at the hotel bar late and in my pajamas. Mason, Kingston, and Jones were sitting at a dimly lit table in the corner. There were only a handful of other people in the place—a couple sitting in a far booth, nuzzling into each other, and a few loners at the bar top.

I went up to the guys' table and Mason immediately started laughing at my pajamas. I was wearing a cropped tank top and long shorts. The matching set was blue, fluffy, and covered with little white clouds. I did a twirl in my thick socks, showing off the outfit, then collapsed in the empty chair between him and Kingston, Jones across from me.

"Shut up," I said. "I'm cozy."

"You look it," Jones said with a playful smirk.

The boys were in simple shorts and t-shirts. Lame. At least one of us had some flair.

"Hey. She won us the game today. She can wear whatever she wants," Kingston said. I snapped and pointed at him in victory.

I was about to launch into some childish taunting, but a waiter showing up stopped the chirps from escaping my mouth.

"What can I get for you, ma'am?" the kid asked. He looked about my age, but his wide eyes and floppy hair gave him an air of innocence.

I ordered a glass of red wine.

"Wine?" Jones asked with amused judgment as the kid left. The boys each had a light beer in front of them, but I hadn't seen any of them take a sip yet.

"What? And your pissy bread juice is better? I don't think so, and you know wine has more alcohol and fewer calories than beer, right?"

"Touché," Jones relented, taking a sip of his bread juice.

I looked at Kingston. He had a barely touched plate of fries in front of him. *Hmmm...*

The kid returned with my wine and headed off before I could pay him. Someone must have opened a tab. I let him go, not allowing myself to order a plate of fries like Kingston. I couldn't afford the calories. I snuck another look at Kingston's plate. Well, maybe a couple wouldn't hurt, right? I took a contemplative sip of wine.

"It was a good game today, Warren," Jones said, bringing my attention away from the plate of calories a foot away.

I perked up at the mention of hockey. "I know, right? Did you see that shot Mason made in the third? I'm surprised Barrett's ankles weren't broken."

"Yeah, that was sick," Jones cheered. For Ethan Jones' big size and intimidating play style, he was a giant teddy bear and a supportive captain. He had trouble with his volume control and ended up shouting more than talking when he got excited, his face lighting up like a freaking Christmas tree. He reached over the table to give

Mason some knuckles. It looked like Mason had forgiven Jones.

Kingston was watching this all with a fond smile on his face, and while he was distracted, I slid my hand across the table and snagged one of his fries. I stuffed it in my mouth, chewed, and swallowed as fast as I could. No one noticed a thing.

"How about you, Riles?" Mason asked. "How was playing with McCarthy for the first time?"

"It was awesome. I've wanted to play with her since she got drafted," I said lamely, not able to put the experience into words that would do it justice.

Jones put his elbows on the table and leaned forward, his dark brown eyes staring intently into mine. His serious face only lasted for a second before it cracked and a suggestive smile broke through. I knew what he was going to ask before he even opened his mouth. "You wanted to *play* with her, huh?"

Mason snorted, and Kingston's head whipped to me.

I just rolled my eyes and sipped my wine, a smile tugging at my lips. My old teammates from Seattle had made the same suggestion every time we played against Vancouver as well. Boys were idiots.

"What, you don't think she's hot?" Jones asked in response to my eye roll.

"I think she's gorgeous. You know who also thinks she's gorgeous?" I paused for dramatic effect. "Her girlfriend. Who is an MMA fighter."

The boys grimaced simultaneously, and I laughed.

As the night dragged on, the boys slowly drank their single allotted beers, but I ordered another glass of wine. Unlike them, I wasn't playing tomorrow. Still, I didn't want to get trashed. That wouldn't be a good look.

I had just pilfered another fry, threw it into my mouth, and was chewing fast when I made eye contact with Kingston. *Uh-oh.* I swallowed and tried to look innocent. He narrowed his eyes at me then looked at the plate he hadn't touched in thirty minutes. There was a little dent on the side of the fry pile closest to me.

Kingston rolled his eyes but pushed the plate closer to me with a little smile. I beamed at him and grabbed two more, my diet temporarily out the window. Come to me, salty goodness.

I made a few more dents as conversation flowed smoothly between everyone.

We must have been talking for a couple hours or so when an alarm suddenly went off on Mason's phone, interrupting Jones' story about his rookie year. Mason grabbed his cell off the table, jolting out of his chair as if it had electrocuted him. His chair squeaked across the tile floor, and we all looked at him in question.

His fingers turned white around his phone, and he shifted on his feet. "I—I have to go," he stuttered, shuffling backward.

Wait a minute; I recognized that stupid look on his face. I cocked my head, and when he met my gaze, I saw his eyes filled with shy excitement. It looked like someone had a phone date scheduled.

"Well, go and get out of here then," I said, waving him out. He smiled down at me gratefully, kissed the top of my head, then practically ran to the hotel elevators without another word.

"Well, okay then," Jones said. "I guess I'll head back to my room also. Although, I'll do it less weirdly." He finished off the rest of his beer, which must have been disgustingly warm by now. "Y'all coming up too?"

"In a second," I said. "I have to finish off Kingston's fries first."

Kingston chuckled. "I'll be up there in a few. Gotta settle the tab."

Suddenly, Jones leaned toward Kingston and dropped his voice. "If you're a couple hours past curfew, I won't tell." He must have seen my confused look because Jones' eyes shifted pointedly. I followed his glance and found a gorgeous redhead sitting at the bar top, a beer bottle in her hand.

I met her gaze and was shocked. Beautiful green eyes sat in an equally stunning face. Her face was slim and defined, with perfect, make-up-less glass skin. She was breath-taking. She was exactly my type, almost the spitting image of one of my ex-girlfriends, but I clearly wasn't her type. No, she only had eyes for Sebastian Kingston.

Mood ruined, I turned back to the table, putting the redhead behind me, and stuffed a handful of fries in my mouth, fighting off the inappropriate feeling rising in me. *Nope, nope, nope.* While I was focused on the cold, limp fries and my erratic emotions, Kingston must have said something because Jones nodded his head at Kingston and left with a lot less ruckus than Mason.

"I think it's your fault," Kingston said conversationally.

Taking a shallow breath, I shoved the last soggy fry into my mouth and picked my head up.

I was immediately under a microscope. Kingston's head was cocked, a tornado of unnamable emotions flickering across his face as he studied me. I froze under the eyes of a watchful predator, afraid of what he might see in my face.

"What?" I asked nervously.

He stared at me for a moment more, picking up his empty beer bottle and spinning it between his hands. "Mason. He wasn't this weird until you showed up."

A short laugh burst out of me at the unexpected comment, and I collapsed against the back of my chair at the break in the tension. "He *is* a weirdo, huh?"

Mason's exit had been less than graceful but, considering the circumstances that only I was privy to, completely understandable

"That's the thing; he's not usually. He's been this serious machine since he was drafted. He's all hockey, all the time," Kingston said, his voice light, but his gaze still intense on my face. "It's kind of stressful to watch. He's so determined to prove himself."

"But he has proven himself, right?"

"Yeah, he has. And he still is. But now it looks like he's having fun. Jones kept trying to loosen him up a little, but he wasn't having much luck. Then you show up, and it's like there's new life in him. It's not just his personality either. He's even been playing better these last couple games. You said you guys grew up together, and I've seen how close you are. Hell, he was at your house when I picked you up yesterday. He's practically your family, right? Why?"

"He's my soulmate," I said without hesitation. Kingston furrowed his brow, so I elaborated. "From the second I met him, it felt like I'd known him my whole life. We were with each other all the time and still are. I've talked to him every single day for the past nine years. That's more than I talk to my brother. At this point, Mason knows me better than I know myself. Hell, he's the reason I'm still playing hockey."

"What do you mean?"

"Well, after my parents died, I never wanted to put on a pair of skates ever again. It just didn't feel right without them in the stands, cheering me on. But Mason pulled me out of my house and threw me out onto a rink because he knew I needed it. He's always been there for me, just like I'll always be there for him."

"And you make each other better players."

I nodded. "Exactly."

Silence stretched, then, "You really love hockey."

I scrunched my eyebrows at Kingston. It wasn't a question, but I answered anyway. "Of course I do. Why else would I be here?"

Kingston hummed and flicked at the peeling label of his bottle. "Yeah."

Suddenly, a sea of Chanel perfume passed us. The redhead had moved from the bar and was taking a seat at a table a few yards away. She flipped her scarlet hair and settled into a chair that allowed her the perfect view of our table and the man at it.

The woman didn't escape Kingston's notice, but he didn't acknowledge her either.

I narrowed my eyes at her. My un-team-mate-like feelings toward Kingston and my competitive nature were being spurred on by the wine. It was probably time to get out of here.

Kingston must have had the same thought. "Guess it's time to go up. Some of us have a game to play tomorrow."

I snorted, and we got up. Kingston settled the tab at the bar while being watched by piercing green eyes. Seconds later, he was back, and I thanked him for the drinks as we made our way to the elevator, my body swaying a little more than I anticipated. I wasn't drunk, but I wasn't completely sober. A pleasant fluidity filled my limbs as we came to a stop at the elevator doors.

He pushed the call button, and I looked at him while we waited. His face was relaxed, the exact opposite of the haughty, scrunched face I met him with.

"What's up?" he asked.

"I thought you were an asshole." *Whoops.* "But you're not," I rushed out, blushing a little. Dear God, I was losing control of my mouth.

Then Sebastian Kingston threw back his head and laughed—loud and full-bodied. My jaw fell open unattractively as he continued. Wow. I'd just made The King laugh. Something like that deserved a medal, right?

Eventually, Kingston's laughter settled down and I picked my jaw off the floor, but I couldn't take my eyes off him. He should have more fun. He really did have a captivating smile. And his five o'clock shadow was nice too; the short dark stubble contrasted beautifully against his skin and brought out the pink of his lips.

The elevator opened in front of us. I tore my eyes away from his face. *Damn it, Warren.*

We went inside and hit our floor numbers— fifteen and sixteen.

"When I first met you, I thought you were an air-head," he said, his face still filled with mirth.

I gasped. "What? What would make you think…?" Oh, wait. The first time I met him, I was standing shirtless and braless in the middle of the locker room. Heat devoured my face. "I guess that wasn't the best first impression, was it?" I fought the urge to hide my face in my hands. "It was defiantly memorable, at least. Don't worry. I realized I was wrong rather quickly. Although…" He gave my outfit a pointed once over. "Excuse me. These pajamas are fantastic. And look at these socks!" I stepped into his space and pointed at my feet, covering my embarrassment with playful indignation. "They are both cute and comfortable."

He looked down at my Hello Kitty-clad feet, and I wiggled my toes, making the fluffy cats dance to the soft elevator music.

"See!" I looked up from my feet in triumph and paused.

I was right underneath him.

His eyes bored into mine. *God, they are beautiful.* The grey stood in stark contrast against his black, wavy hair and pulled me in. They searched my eyes then flicked down to my lips. His pupils grew rapidly, almost blotting out the grey. I licked my lips nervously. He copied me, his pink tongue leaving his lips glistening.

I slowly went onto my tiptoes, swaying as if in a trance. Then his mouth parted, and I crashed lips onto his. His hands caught me around my waist as I fell into him, and he took a step back under my sudden weight. His back hit the wall, and the elevator shook around us.

His mouth was warm and tasted of beer. I loved it.

I licked into his mouth, and his tongue met mine. My arms locked around his neck as he crushed me closer to him.

Suddenly, he spun us around, trading places. I leaned into the elevator wall eagerly, pulling him with me until not even a millimeter of air was between us. One of his hands dropped and groped at my bare thigh. I lifted it and wrapped it around his hip. His muscles flexed, and then I was sitting on the handrail encircling the elevator.

With one hand, I scratched across his neck and dug my nails into his jaw, short hair tickling my fingers. My mouth opened wider to fully receive his tongue. He growled lightly, and my eyes fluttered under their lids.

The elevator dinged, and my eyes snapped open. It was like I was plunged into an ice bath. Reason flooded back into me.

Fuck.

I dropped my leg from him immediately and ducked out of his grip. The elevator was on my floor. I sent up a quick thanks that no one was in the hallway as I watched Kingston heave for breath, his eyes on the floor and his hands clenching at his sides as if missing my body.

I backed away slowly until I was standing between the doors of the elevators.

"Shit, shit, shit," I mumbled in horror. That— that shouldn't have happened.

Then Kingston lifted his head, and my stomach squeezed. His eyes drilled into me, searching. I stared back and bit my lip, waiting for him to say something. He didn't. His gaze dropped to my mouth, and I realized my lower lip was being worried between my teeth. I let it go and clenched my jaw.

Still silent, Kingston touched his lips, still staring at mine, then wiped away the wetness at the corners of his mouth.

I clenched my jaw harder. He was watching me like we were on the ice and he was trying to sneak a puck past me, reading my every twitch, trying to see inside my head.

The elevator sounded again, and the doors tried to close on me. They bounced off my shoulders and jolted me out of my stasis.

A second later, they tried to close again, but I stuck my arm out, holding them open. I needed to say something; I couldn't just leave it like this. Whatever "this" was.

Unfortunately, "I'm sorry," was all that came out.

Great job, Warren. So eloquent.

Kingston finally opened his mouth, and I held my breath. "So, you're not—"

Crap. On second thought, I was not ready for this. I let go of the elevator and stepped back. He could have stopped them again, but he didn't. I watched as the doors closed between us, finally cutting me off from that calculating stare.

My relief only lasted until I walked down the hall to my room, scanned the key card, and closed my door behind me. Then the panic came back in full force.

Fuck. Fuck! FUCK! What did I just do? No, no, no.

I couldn't call Mason. He was either asleep or on the phone with Drew. So I paced. I paced enough to feel a light burn in my calves then collapsed onto the bed.

My blanket cocoon didn't erase my mistakes, and I fell asleep replaying my kiss with Kingston over and over again in my head.

9

I prayed that I would wake up with the worst hangover known to mankind. I wanted a brain-bursting, vomiting-inducing pounding in my head that would knock out a fully grown elephant. Because then I could say that I was drunk off my ass last night. I had no such luck. There wasn't so much as a twinge of pain behind my eyes. Turns out I wasn't a drunken idiot, I was just a regular idiot. Fuck.

I groaned and rolled around in bed for a minute, wallowing, before I forced myself up and into the shower. Once dressed in one of my game-day pantsuits and rocking some confidence-boosting heels, I packed in five seconds, grabbed my luggage, and left for what was sure to be an awkward day.

I strode to Mason's room to retrieve him, and we quickly headed out, suitcases rolling behind us.

"So, how was your date with Drew?" I asked him when we were in the elevator. This damn elevator! I stayed to the left as we descended, away from the spot on the wall I had been pressed against the night before and the memory of soft lips and hard hands that it brought. My fingers twitched as if they could still feel Kingston's rough stubble underneath them. I needed to get out of here. Thankfully, the team was leaving straight from the arena to the airport after the game, so we weren't coming back to the hotel.

"It wasn't a date," Mason protested, but his smile gave him away.

Despite my internal turmoil, I bumped him with my hip. At least one of our love lives wasn't a complete disaster.

But any joy I felt for my best friend and brother was immediately crushed by overwhelming anxiety as we stepped off the elevator. I instinctively grabbed onto Mason's arm and squeezed. As subtly as I could, I looked around the busy lobby to see if Kingston was there. He wasn't, but I didn't relax as Mason and I headed toward the bus that was going to take us to the arena. It was only a matter of time before I ran into him.

"What's up, Riles?" Mason asked.

"Nothing. What's up with you? Tell me everything about your not-date. Well, not everything. I don't need to hear about my brother having phone sex."

"There was no phone sex," Mason whisper-shouted into my ear as we passed a group of businessmen. I chuckled under my breath. "Especially not with my roommate sleeping five feet from me," he continued. "We just talked."

"About?" I hedged.

Mason shrugged. "I don't know. Everything? About the game. About life. About his work. He's reconnecting with a lot of his old classmates." He paused, and I looked up at him. He was chewing on his lip. He met my eyes for a second then looked forward, something weird swirling in his eyes. "He's thinking about moving back to New York."

My mouth dropped open, and I wanted to question him, but we had reached the bus.

Drew hadn't mentioned anything about relocating. Hell, it had only been a few years since he moved to Los Angeles. With a few strings pulled through connections he had made at NYU, he got a job at one of the most prestigious finance companies on the west coast. Last we spoke about his work, he seemed to be enjoying the company and was climbing the corporate ladder fast. I could only think of a couple reasons why he would want to move back to New York, the main one being the man next to me.

Mason and I threw our suitcases into the bus storage area then boarded and took our seats in the middle of the bus. Mason, as usual, took the window seat, and I quickly searched the bus. Kingston hadn't boarded yet.

Careful of the ears around us, I ducked my head as close to Mason as could with being on top of him. "When did he start thinking about this?"

Mason shrugged and curled into his coat, burying his fists into the pockets. As out of the blue as this news was, I would have thought Mason would be over the moon. He had been in love with Drew forever. I didn't understand why he wasn't bouncing off the walls.

"Excuse me, Warren."

Ethan Jones' voice whipped my head up. Jones was working his big body through the aisle. I squeezed my legs farther into my row to let him pass, then found myself looking up into the narrowed eyes of Sebastian Kingston.

Kingston's eye twitched as he looked suspiciously between me and Mason, still cuddled together. His thoughts were clear on his face, and I almost flinched back in disgust.

Oh, God no. Ughh. I was quick to silently shake my head at Kingston, hoping my near-vomit expression conveyed to him just how *not* together Mason and I were.

Thankfully, Kingston seemed to get the message. His face smoothed out, and he moved past us, not saying anything.

"I'm not sure about this, Riles." Mason's whisper brought me back to our conversation.

"About what, Mase?"

His lips were pursed as he glared at his lap. The man that was practically busting with love a day ago was the very antithesis of happiness now.

133

He sighed and finally looked up. His usually soft, blue eyes were terrified. "About everything. We haven't even gone on a date yet, but Drew's ready to move back across the country." Suddenly, Mason peeked his head over our seats and checked up and down the bus as the last of the players boarded. Then he ducked back down and lowered his voice until it was nearly inaudible. "You know what he told me last night? He told me he's been in love with me for years. Years!" he hissed incredulously. "Did you know that, Riles?"

I hesitated for a minute then nodded. Mason reared back, a look of betrayal coming over his face. I grabbed his arm desperately. "I'm sorry, Mase," I whispered. "He told me not to tell you about his feelings years ago. Just like you told me not to tell him. But I don't see what the problem is. Now you both know, so shouldn't you be happy?"

Mason's mouth dropped open. "Happy? I'm scared as fuck. It's one thing to have feelings, but love doesn't mean a relationship is going to work out. Honestly, I kind of want him to stay in California. At least that way, with all the long distance, we could see what this thing is instead of jumping into the deep end with no backup plan. This is just moving quickly. It's going to fuck up our family if it ends badly."

I squeezed him. "But, Mase, what if it never ends?"

"I don't see how it can't."

I wanted to comfort him some more, but I'd known Mason for years, and I knew when he just needed space. I gave his arm one last squeeze then let go.

He grimaced at me then pulled out earbuds from his pocket. I copied him, and we spent the short ride to the arena thinking.

Once we got to the rink, everything was hectic. The team quickly grabbed breakfast from the kitchen staff, got changed, and went to morning skate. A couple hours later, everyone sat for a game meeting then broke apart to shower, kill time, or prepare for the game. Except for the silent exchange on the bus, I'd managed to not make eye contact with Sebastian Kingston for the whole morning, avoiding the drills I could feel burrowing into the side of my face from his direction.

Usually, Mason would have asked what was wrong, but he was dealing with his own things. Not that you could tell by his performance during practice. After a fast shower, Mason took off to run through his pre-game routine. Since I wasn't scheduled to play today, I skipped my usual mediation and visualization and saw one of the team's masseuses. For forty-five minutes, my mind was blessedly quiet as Neil worked out my knots and relieved the muscle soreness from yesterday's game.

But the quiet didn't last for long. I was wobbling out of the physical therapy rooms, feeling like a wet spaghetti noodle, when a streak of distinct black hair flashed in my peripherals. With the reactions that I'd honed for the past decade of my life, I pivoted around the corner before Kingston could see me. As I pressed into the wall, hoping it would swallow me and hide me from the world, any relaxation I felt disintegrated and my shoulders drew up to my ears, my back a fresh plane of tension.

I sighed and knocked the back of my head against the concrete wall. This was ridiculous. Still, I waited a full minute before peeking around the corner and leaving my hiding spot when the coast was clear.

I needed to chill. Thankfully, I knew just where to go.

I quickly found the gym and dropped onto the mats next to a couple of my teammates, music pounding away in my ears. I went a little harder on my stretching routine than I usually would, but the deep burn helped me tune out the world.

Honestly, I should just talk to Kingston. This avoiding game was less than a day old and was already exhausting. I didn't have the time to be playing cat and mouse with him. I already had enough to worry about without being on the lookout for him everywhere I went.

I had to end this little stand-off soon. It was going to be awkward as hell, but I didn't have any other choice. This weirdness was my fault, so I was going to have to take my medicine, apologize, grit my teeth through his "it's not you, it's me" speech, then, hopefully, we could go back to being normal friends. Or as close to that as we could get.

With a deep sigh, I leaned farther into my last stretch, the pike pulling at my hamstrings until they felt like they were going to snap. I had to wait until after the game to talk to Kingston; our team couldn't afford to have its best left wing distracted. And I didn't want to air out dirty laundry in Vancouver's very echoey arena.

Tentative plan made, I popped off the mats and claimed one of the free treadmills on the other side of the gym. I set a light pace, going more for distance than time, and jogged along with the beat of my music.

A couple miles in, someone joined me on the treadmill to my left. I looked over to find Alex fucking Lukin beside me. Great.

He smirked at me. I tried to fight off an eye roll, but it managed to slip through when he increased his speed, his stare practically daring me to compete. He shouldn't have done that. I was being more aggressive than usual because I was trying to work through some shit, but unlike me, Lukin had a game to play in a couple hours. He needed to take it easy, or he would wear himself out before he even put a skate on the ice.

I held steady, but Lukin kept on increasing his speed. I gave him a look but didn't say anything; I wasn't his mother. Once I hit the three-mile mark, I got off, and Lukin looked triumphant.

Whatever, bud. I let him think he won something and went to scrounge up some tennis balls from my locker.

On the way there, I walked by a spread that the cooks had laid out in the dining area and made a detour. The buffet table was piled with a variety of food and snacks. I unwrapped and stuffed half a granola bar in my mouth while I contemplated which sandwich to choose. The turkey looked good, but so did the chicken and avocado. I shoved the rest of the granola bar in my mouth and chewed. *Hmmm...*

"Warren," a voice said behind me, and granola lodged in my throat. *Son of a bitch.*

I shot around as Kingston closed the door to the room and leaned against it. Trapped.

Eyes wide and watering, I coughed around my granola bar. After a couple tries, the piece choking me worked its way out of my esophagus, but my mouth was still full, cheeks round like a hamster.

"We need to talk," he said, his face blank. *Damn this man! Show some emotion on your face!* He was completely stoic. He was in "King" mode.

I chewed the dry-as-hell bar as fast as I could and tried to swallow it, but the granola was not having it. *Fuck it. Time for charades.*

I held up my finger and swirled it around, trying to encompass the whole rink in my gesture, and shook my head.

"Not at work?" Kingston asked, trying to decipher my shitty mimes.

I nodded aggressively.

A sigh broke his flat face, and he walked up to me. His hand reached toward me, and I froze. Reaching around me, he grabbed a water bottle from the table and shoved it into my hands. "Soon. Tonight."

He waited for me to nod again then left, closing the door behind him. Free from the overwhelming presence of Sebastian Kingston, I finally managed to swallow the granola and washed it down with the water. Shit, I really needed to avoid enclosed spaces with Kingston. They got me in trouble.

I grabbed a chicken and avocado sandwich, waited a minute, then got the hell out of there.

"You saved us, Warren!" Jones enveloped me in a hug. I held my breath so the overpowering smell of sweaty man-body wouldn't knock me out and hugged him back. He jiggled me in his arms until Kingston came up behind him and clapped him on the back.

"Don't kill her, man, or she won't be able to save our asses again."

Jones laughed and released me to go to his locker. I was nervous to look up at Kingston, but he just nodded at me with approval, not a hint of anything more than coworker-like support on his face. He moved to his cubby before I could throw off the unexpected wave of disappointment and muster up a response.

A couple guys patted me on the back as they passed, chatting amicably. The team's mood had improved dramatically since the end of the second period. Not only had we won, but there wasn't a pissed-off goalie throwing shit across the locker room.

Lukin had the game on lock in the first period; he was in the zone and on his way to his first NHL shutout. But, during the second period, Vancouver got a puck past him, and Lukin couldn't recover. He ran out of steam trying to overcompensate, and by the end of the period, he had let in two more goals. Coach Hansson probably would have kept him in the game ... if he hadn't marched into the locker room after the period and chucked his mask across the room, leaving a huge dent in the wall. I hadn't had time to wonder who would pay for that because, in the next second, Coach benched Lukin and I was put in.

Unlike my first game with them, I was able to help pull the team out of the red. I didn't let in any more goals, and our forwards suddenly had a fire lit under their asses. We took the game back and didn't even have to go into overtime.

X

I received a few more nods from the boys and a sharp high five from Mason as I sat down at my assigned cubby to strip off my pads. Once I was down to my sports bra and underwear, I unraveled the platinum braids I wore under my headgear and took off for the showers. My short amount of time on the ice didn't allow me to work up a big sweat, but I had an even sheen of stickiness covering my body that I was eager to get off.

As I stepped around Jones on my way, I felt, more than saw, Kingston's eyes glue themselves to my barely dressed figure. His equally bare body flirted at the side of my vision, and I struggled to keep a straight face and not make eye contact with him over Jones' shoulder.

I would have been able to ignore him before. Before the elevator. Before I knew how hot his tongue was when it slid against mine. Before it felt like my body knew the moment he stepped into a room.

Since high school, I had been surrounded by half-naked, good-looking, muscular men, but I had a hard-and-fast rule to not stare. It wasn't always easy, but I used my perceived sexuality as a shield. Any accidental stray eyes were brushed away with the excuse that I was gay. It was a system I'd used for my entire career, and it had worked out flawlessly until I met Sebastian fucking Kingston.

I had tried to keep my eyes off of him, but temptation was a strong opponent. I knew

Kingston caught me looking when we were in the locker room alone. Had I managed to be more professional, he may have brushed it off entirely. Then the elevator happened.

Now I had to explain my bullshit to him. I could basically kiss his respect and our fledgling friendship goodbye.

I made it into the showers, turned the water to ice cold, and scrubbed down viciously.

As the bus pulled up and parked in the Snow Globe lot, a wave of relief crashed over me. We were finally home. Thank God. Vancouver had been rough on my mind. With all the drama, I couldn't even fully enjoy our wins.

The whole reason for letting people think I was a lesbian was to cause less drama, but I went and fucked that right up, didn't I? After the excruciatingly long plane and bus ride back to the arena, I didn't care that it was two in the morning. I was more than ready to talk to Kingston and get the inevitable awkward conversation out of the way.

I nudged Mason awake. It had been a bumpy ride from the airport, yet Mason had passed out immediately and hadn't stirred for anything. Typical.

We grabbed our backpacks and got off the bus in a crowd of zombie-like hockey players. Road trips were hard for everyone, and we all just wanted to go home and crash. Everyone but me and Kingston, that was. While the team got their luggage from the bus carriage, Kingston came up to me, a pointed look on his face.

I sighed and moved off to the side of the crowd. He must be eager to get the "you're an amazing girl, but I just don't see you that way" speech over as well.

"We can't be seen leaving together," I mumbled to him. "I rode with Mason here, so follow us to my house. We can talk there."

He nodded then went into the mass of players and grabbed his suitcase.

I was about to wade into the fray myself when Mason popped up beside me, both our bags in his hands. He glanced curiously at Kingston's retreating back. Mason wasn't stupid or blind; despite being distracted by his relationship problems, he knew I was hiding something.

"Thanks, Mase. Hey, do you mind if I drive?" I asked, taking my suitcase from him and popping up the handle.

Mason shot me a questioning look but fished his keys out of his pocket and handed them over. "Sure."

Once at his green monstrosity of a Jeep, we threw our bags in the back, and I claimed the driver's seat. I needed a little bit of distraction from this conversation, and I didn't trust Mason not to crash us in surprise when I spilled my secrets.

"So ... something happened last night," I started.

"No shit, Riles. You've been weird as fuck all day. What the hell did you do?"

I pulled his giant car out of the parking spot and made my way down the aisle slowly. Kingston's truck lights appeared behind me, and I drove out of the lot, taking a deep breath as I launched into my story, telling him everything that happened last night and today.

Thankfully, I lived close to the rink, and as I pulled into Mason's usual spot behind my car, he was just winding down from his storm of questions. In the rearview mirror, Kingston parked behind me and killed his lights.

"Is that Kingston behind us?" Mason asked, finally noticing our tail. *Note to self: Mason would die immediately in a spy movie.*

"I have to go face the music."

I hopped out to get my bags, and Mason followed to grab his own.

"You staying here tonight?" I asked.

"Yeah," he answered and jerked his head to the right. Drew's car was parked in front of mine. Ah. "Do you got this, Riles? You need some backup?"

I smiled tightly. "Nah. I got it, but can you take this inside?"

Mason took my suitcase, but I kept my backpack. Then he went to the door, took one last look back, and disappeared inside.

Time to get this over with.

I marched to Kingston's car, opened the door, having heard the locks click, and planted myself in the passenger's seat. "Okay."

Surprisingly, instead of immediately bursting out with questions, he put his car into gear and drove. Guess we were going somewhere. I had expected to just talk in his car. Not arguing, I buckled my belt as Kingston headed … farther down my street? *What?*

A minute later, my question was answered when he parked in front of a brownstone a street away from mine. It was almost a mirror of my house, except it didn't have the rose bushes that my father had planted in front of mine. We got out, and I gaped at his house as he grabbed his bags from his truck. "You live a minute from me?"

"I guess I forgot to mention that earlier," he said casually and went to the door. I followed behind, stunned.

That was so weird. I'd never seen him or his car around, but to be fair, I'd only been back in town for less than a week. Though that was more than enough time to gain and lose the first friend I'd made in hockey since Mason.

Kingston unlocked his house, stepped inside, threw his bags off to the side, and held open the door to the lion's den for me. How kind.

10

*K*ingston guided me into his house, and it was like looking into a funhouse mirror. His house had the same layout as mine. But where mine was filled with things and memories from my childhood, his was decorated with modern furniture and was spotless. It was more than a little jarring.

I stopped under the arch separating the living area and the foyer and leaned against it, wanting to stay close to the door.

Mirroring me, Kingston propped his hip against his black cotton sectional. His suit, just as dark as his couch, sat on him like a second skin, emphasizing his broad shoulder and cutting sharply to his waist. He crossed his arms over his chest, and I was thrown back to when we first met, him staring me down and trying to get a read. I couldn't even begin to guess what he was getting off me. Hell, *I* barely knew what I was feeling.

He, in turn, was as stoic as a king.

The silence only lasted a few moments before I broke it, wanting to get this over. I stood up straight, channeling all the power that my fierce, navy pantsuit and sharp stilettos gave me, and let the words rush out of me like water through a dam. "We don't need to do this. Trust me, I get it, and I'm sorry. I'm sorry I kissed you and put you in an awkward position. You don't need to let me down gently. It won't happen again, and we can go back to being friends."

He cocked his head. "Friends? Is that what you want?"

I paused. No, I didn't want to be friends with him; I wanted to be more. But that wasn't happening in this lifetime, so I would just have to suck it up and settle. "Yeah? I mean, ideally? If you can get over this and if we can move on. That's why I'm here, right?"

Again, he just stood there, his brain working behind his eyes.

I hated this. Hated not being able to read him. I read people for a living! I knew when someone was coming straight at me or when they were going for a deke. I could tell what any given player would do based on their play style and past actions. It was my job, and I was damn good at it. But staring at Kingston was like staring at a brick wall. Except this brick wall was studying me just as intently as I it. It was driving me crazy, and I wanted to claw out his pretty little eyes!

Say something, damnit!

"So, you're not a lesbian?"

I blinked, the abrupt change letting most of the wind out of my sails. "Um ... no. Not entirely. I'm bisexual."

He hummed curiously. "Then why aren't you out as bisexual? Wouldn't that have been just as easy as coming out as gay?"

No, it wouldn't have been. "Do you know when being gay in professional sports is actually beneficial? When you're a woman on an all-male team," I answered before he could guess and took up pacing across his living room.

His gaze followed me as I went back and forth, trying my hardest to put this into words.

"My teammates in high school were kind of dicks. Thankfully, I wasn't changing with them, so I didn't have to deal with their shit while half-naked in front of them. On the ice, when Mason was away from me, some of them got sexual though. It was harassment, and looking back, I should have reported it, but I didn't want to cause more drama on the team. I just ignored it. Then, during my sophomore year, I got a girl-friend. Her name was Kara, and she was the sweetest person I'd ever met. She was the first person I ever dated; I didn't have a lot of friends, and there was no way I was going to get with one of the Neanderthals on the team. Of course, I wanted to keep it secret, but you know how that shit goes; everyone knew the next day. At first, I was nervous. Not only was I the only girl on the team, but now I was the only out queer person too. I was dreading going to practice, but the weirdest thing happened. They quit with the shitty jokes. I mean, they didn't stop completely; that's impossible. But no one was flirting with me or asking me if I liked what I saw. It was like I became one of the guys overnight."

"So, you stuck with it."

"Yeah. I even became friends with some of their girlfriends because they knew I wasn't trying to steal their boyfriends. It was weird, but it worked, so I just rolled with it. And it's still working now. None of the guys here or in Seattle has ever tried to flirt with me. I have yet to get a question from the press about which teammate I think is cutest or who has the best ass or biggest dick."

Kingston's lip twitched. "Berk has the biggest dick."

Laughter burst out of my chest suddenly, and I stopped pacing to throw Kingston a smirk. "On *this* team, sure, but Marcus Castillo would put him to shame."

"Really?"

"Oh, yeah. I accidentally got a peek in Seattle and was honestly terrified." My laughter turned into light chuckles as I remembered Mason's reaction when I told him.

"Accidentally?"

"Of course. I don't look at teammates in the lock—" I stopped short, remembering why I was at Kingston's house in the first place. He noticed my pause, of course, and shoved off the couch to stand straight, dropping his arms to his side. "Except for me."

I didn't say a thing.

There was about eight feet separating us, and while Kingston didn't step any closer, the air between us shrank until it was as if he was standing inches away, watching every flicker of my eye or twitch of my face. "Are you into me, Warren?"

I grimaced at my feet. *Fuck.*

"You are," he said. It wasn't a question.

I talked to my black Louboutin pumps, focusing on my pink-painted toes that peeked out the front instead of the immovable force in front of me. "Don't worry. We can go back to being teammates. I didn't mean to drag you into this. I'm sure you've had to deal with shit like this before. You don't need to let me down easy. My feelings will go away."

"Let you down easy? Why would I do that?"

My chin dug into my chest. I guessed he did need to make this a little painful. Make sure he didn't leave me with any hope. I understood. Bracing, I waited.

When he next spoke, his voice was closer than before. I was so startled by the deep rumbling of his voice that it took me a second to register what he said. "I like you too."

I snapped my head up. He had moved closer, and his grey eyes pierced my soul from only a couple feet away. "Wha—what did you say?

Are you fucking with me right now? Because that's cruel."

He threw his hands up in exasperation. "Of course, I'm not fucking with you, Warren! I would never do that."

I squinted at him. No, he wouldn't do that, would he? I hadn't known him that long, but I knew he would never be that cruel. He was serious. He liked me. Like he *liked* liked me. The second I thought it, I wanted to smack myself. What was wrong with me? Was I going to ask him to hold my hand on the way to the bus next? Leave a note in his locker? Check yes or no.

He continued. "Ever since that first fucking game. Anybody else would have quit, then and there. Hell, *I* probably would have, but you just kept on smiling. We threw you to the wolves, but you didn't care. You were having fun. I honestly wasn't sure if you were just taunting us or if you were actually fucking crazy."

"Did you come to a conclusion?" Even in my shock, I couldn't help teasing him.

"I'm pretty sure it was a little bit of both."

"It was. You bunch of assholes didn't even know. I would have faced down SEAL team six on skates if it meant I got to play on that ice."

And I meant it. Playing by myself was amazing. I played against a whole team of NHL players all by myself. I definitely wasn't fantastic, letting in more than a few pucks, but it would probably be one of the defining moments of my career. I didn't know if I could ever top that.

"Well, it was damn hot. You just stared me down, all sweaty and worn out but still smiling. I swear I got hard in the middle of the ice." Most guys would have been ashamed to admit that, but Kingston looked like he was reveling in the memory.

I snorted. "Well, sorry about that."

He finally closed the last of the distance between us until we stood chest to chest in the middle of his living room, my heels allowing our eyes to meet on an equal level. "You should be. You've been driving me insane this past week. I thought I was losing it. Sometimes I could have sworn that you were flirting with me, but I knew you couldn't have been. I was so confused and half convinced that I was hallucinating the looks you gave me. I mean, you didn't like men, and I was trying so damn hard to not be a creep. It's borderline impossible when you wear those tiny fucking panties in the locker room though. Or when you chirp at me over ice cream. Or kiss me in elevators. It's impossible not to fall for that."

The grey orbs that were always stone on the ice, full of determination, were now filled with desire. My breath hitched. We shouldn't be doing this. We were teammates.

I leaned toward him as if pulled by gravity. He caught me by the waist, just like he did in the elevator then ... nothing. Our lips paused inches apart, breaths heaving between us. He was waiting for me. This would have to be my decision.

I gripped his biceps in desperation, fighting for one more second, then gave in and plunged my hands into his hair. I pulled him to me, and we clashed together, mouths greeting each other as if they had missed being separate for so long.

He grunted deeply as our tongues entangled, and a desire that had been building since we met exploded from me. I tore my hand from his hair and groped at his jacket with an impatient whine. He got the message and tugged it off but didn't stop there. He unbuttoned his charcoal shirt, and I helped pull it down his arm.

Fuck, he was gorgeous. I stroked his tattoo-covered torso, marveling at how solid it was. I had forgotten how hard the male body was. I pressed into his abs. They had no give. *Oh my God.*

His hands immediately returned to my waist and pulled me close, so he could rain down gentle kisses on my neck. I jerked backward, ripping him from my neck. A confused sound left him but was quickly silenced as I ripped my jacket off and stripped off my blouse. He didn't seem to care that my sports bra smushed down my boobs as he returned my earlier favor and ran his hands down my torso.

"Gorgeous," he breathed out, petting my stomach.

I let him touch for a second before I stepped back again. We had somewhere to be.

"Bedroom?" I asked.

"Upstairs."

He grabbed my hand, and we booked it to his room.

The layout of the top half of his brownstone was slightly different from mine, but I didn't get a chance to look around because as soon as we stepped inside his bedroom, he was on me.

He pushed me up against the wall beside the door, and it was the elevator all over again. Our mouths devoured each other as he drew up my leg around his hips. I pulled myself up by his shoulder, brought up my other leg to wrap around his waist, and locked my ankles. Hanging onto him, I kicked off my heels into a far corner. I didn't think Kingston even noticed, as distracted by my tongue as he was.

He eventually pulled away when the need for oxygen became too strong, my legs still wrapped around him. My boobs undulated under my sports bra with my heaving breaths as I stared at him. God, and he called me gorgeous? Had he ever seen himself in a mirror? He was physical perfection, and the hunger for me in his eyes only set me aflame further.

He pulled away from the wall, turned, and carried me the short distance to his bed, not even flinching from my weight. His legs hit the bed, and he bent at the waist, placing his hands down on either side of me. I knew I was supposed to drop onto the mattress, but I held on, dangling like a spider monkey, and smiled up at him. His back flexed under my hands as he struggled to hold me up. His face strained, but he held firm.

"Nice core," I said and finally let go. I sprawled out on the bed with a laugh, my legs hanging off the mattress.

Kingston let out a quick breath of exertion and kneeled on the floor, glaring at me for my antics.

With an apologetic smile, I sat up, took off my sports bra, and let my tits spring free. Kingston zeroed in on them immediately, hands already reaching up. *Apology accepted.*

I spread my legs farther, and Kingston shuffled forward, hands playing with my tits the entire time. My breasts had never been huge, just barely fitting into a C cup, but they were friendly, and Kingston seemed to enjoy them. He jiggled them in his hands and pinched my nipples. I arched into him, a moan tearing from my throat.

Then he brought his mouth to them and bit a nipple, sending sparks of pleasure and pain through me. He switched between my girls, and I ran my hands through his hair until I couldn't take it anymore. I needed him out of his pants. I traveled down his hard torso until I could tug at the front of his belt.

"Off," I growled. He sat back on his haunches but didn't move fast enough for me. I stretched out a leg, put a foot on his shoulder, and pushed. He got the message and slowly rose, putting me eye to eye with his crotch. I watched in a trance as he shifted his weight to kick off his shoes. Then, with a predatory smile that was more a baring of his teeth, he undid his belt, popped the button on his pants, and drew down his zipper.

His pants and boxer briefs hit the floor, and my jaw followed. *Oh, holy shit.*

My eyes glued to him, I barely noticed my hands moving to take off my pants and panties. The next thing I knew, they were in a pile with his clothes, and we were frozen in place.

"You okay?" Kingston asked. He had been letting me stare at him as I shimmied off my bottoms, but I must have worried him with my silence.

It wasn't like I had never seen a naked man before. Hell, where I worked, it was impossible to avoid them. But I'd never focused on their cocks. It was like my brain didn't process them. Even if I did catch a glimpse, the guys aren't walking around the locker room with hard-ons. Most of them were not that impressive.

Kingston was, though. Kingston was very impressive. About seven and a half inches long and girthy, Kingston's cock was almost identical to my favorite dildo. Except Kingston's had a slight bend that I knew would hit the perfect spot inside of me. I shivered. I couldn't have picked a more perfect penis for my first time. Speaking of...

I tilted my head back to look him in the eye. "I've got to tell you something. I've—uhh—I've never had sex with a guy before."

A loud pause.

Then, "What?"

I stood from the bed, forcing Kingston to take a step back, and held up my hands as if calming a wild animal. "Don't freak out. I'm not a virgin. Haven't been for a while. But—"

Understanding flashed across his face. "But you've only slept with women."

I dropped my hands. "Yeah. I figured you should know."

"...okay. Do you still want to do this?"

"Yes," I said immediately. Sure, he was huge, but there was no way I was backing down from this. My body would turn on me if I even tried.

Kingston reached out and ran his big hockey hands down my arms, the harsh lustful expression fading from his face and being replaced with caution. "Okay. I'll be gentle."

Oh, yeah.

No.

I knocked his hands off me, grabbed him, spun, and shoved him down on the bed. "Oh, there's no need for that," I taunted as I straddled his thighs.

He considered me above him for a moment, then I was the one on my back again and Kingston was smiling evilly above me. Without another word, he dove to me and crushed our mouths together. Feral sounds came from us both as we nipped and bit at each other, giving as good as we got.

I didn't know how long we were lost in the chaos when Kingston tore from my mouth, kissed across my tits, down my abs, and settled between my spread legs. I propped up on my elbows to watch him. He must have sensed my stare because he looked up and rested his chin lightly on my vulva.

"What?"

"Nothing," I said but couldn't help the smile at my train of thought.

His eyes sparkled against his dark stubble and my trimmed curls. He petted my thighs and cocked an eyebrow, wordlessly telling me to go on.

"I'm just curious to see how a man stacks up," I said wryly. "You could say that I have some pretty high standards in this area, and I've heard some not great things about men's abilities."

He finally understood and burst into vicious laughter. "Oh, God. You even chirp in bed," he muttered and stifled his laugh on my inner thigh, his smile so big against me that his teeth scraped skin. I squirmed frantically at the tickling vibrations.

Then I yelped at the sudden pinch on my inner thigh, and Sebastian raised his head, letting my sensitive flesh fall from his pearly whites.

Uh-oh. I knew that look. I had just challenged a professional athlete.

His face disappeared, and I yelped as his tongue went to work. I clawed at the sheet, and he hitched up my legs over his shoulders, digging in. I thrashed about, but he pinned me with a hand on my stomach, not letting up on my pussy.

He added a finger from his free hand and stroked my insides. Then he added another, all the while teasing my clit with the flat of his tongue. A scream pierced the air, and Kingston doubled down.

It didn't take long for me to burst apart, pulling at his sheets as he let me ride out my orgasm on his face. As I came down, I pushed weakly at his head. He dropped my legs from his shoulders and knelt above my slack form.

Smirking down at me, the bastard wiped his chin with the back of his hand, sending a fresh ping of desire through me. "So, how did I stack up?"

Cocky bastard. No way in hell am I telling him that was the fastest and hardest I've ever come.

With more effort than I expected, I regathered my strength and tangled my legs around his hips. Forcing some nonchalance, I smiled sweetly at him and twisted my hips harshly. He slammed to the bed again, and I laughed down at him in triumph. "Ehh, not bad."

His lips still glistened with me, and I pressed my fingertips to them. Hypnotized and horny, I traced his scar. Softly, he kissed my fingers.

My mouth descended for a few quick pecks to his soft, puffy lip. I tasted myself on him and it drove me crazier. Straddling him properly, I aligned my pelvis with his and ground down. He gripped my waist to help me out, and we both moaned as I ground against his cock. It only took a few circles of my hip before I felt myself building up again and becoming desperate.

"Condom."

Kingston, seeming to shake out of a haze, reached into his nightstand, quickly found a box, and came up with a foil square.

I took it and opened it, scooting down to his thighs to free his cock. Quickly, I slid it on and gave his wrapped dick a few pumps, not able to help myself.

With a growl and an aborted hip thrust, Kingston grabbed my wrist and dragged me back up his body, giving me a strong kiss.

I pulled back when I kissed teeth to see him grinning from ear to ear.

"You ready?" he asked.

I smiled back and pushed off his chest. "To break my promise to never have sex with a team-mate? Hell yeah. Hey, I guess you've never slept with a teammate either."

He took ahold of his cock, and I watched as the head parted my lips and settled at the starting line. "No, but I've had a few offers."

His words pulled me away from the delicious sight of us. Before I could ask, he pushed into me, stretching me exquisitely as he bottomed out, and my questions died on a groan.

I fell forward at the fullness of him and had to brace myself against his colorful abs as I got accommodated to his size. When I felt like I could breathe again, my eyes fluttered up, and I was absently glad to see him just as affected as I was. He was caught in the sight of us connecting, his mouth open in awe.

Falling into instinct, I started to rock and threw my head back.

So that's the big deal about cocks, I thought hysterically. *And I thought my dildo was good.*

I might have to throw it away now. Nothing could compare to the feeling of Sebastian's warm, ridged cock plowing into me. I bounced up and down, needing it faster, and circled my hips whenever I got to the bottom.

Kingston kindly helped me out, and with fingers digging into my hips and strong upward thrusts, I was flying high. The next couple hours were a blur of rhythmic slapping, interrupted by moaning, growling, and the occasional scream of ecstasy.

"We have to do that again," came a worn-out voice beside me.

My head fell to the side. I met Sebastian's eyes and nodded with a trembling laugh, too drained and sated to attempt speaking. I knew I had more stamina than most, but Sebastian had put me to shame. Damn athletes. With more effort than I could even think of mustering, Sebastian rolled to his side and threw an arm across my belly.

His eyes trailed over my face, gaze as soft as I'd ever seen it, as he traced circles across my abs. I hummed contentedly. That felt nice.

"Do you want to stay? I mean, it's already five in the morning, but we don't have practice…"

I squinted suspiciously at him. I wasn't fooled by his innocent tone; he was asking for more than a sleepover.

I should say no. I should leave and ignore my feelings for him until they faded away completely. I couldn't afford to risk my career. But…

"On one condition," I said, stone-cold serious. "*No one* can know."

He didn't even hesitate, like he knew that was coming. "Deal."

I studied him until I was satisfied with his earnestness, then cracked a smile. "I mean you're cool and all, but you know what's cooler? Hockey!"

He gasped in outrage and pulled me closer to him.

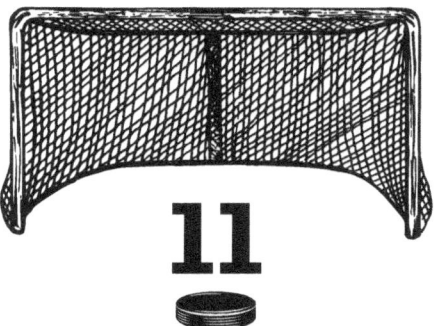

11

The sun was high when I woke, casting painful rays into my eyes. With a groan, I rolled over to escape the light and ran directly into a hard body. *Oh, right.*

Beside me, huddled in his heather grey sheets, Sebastian groaned and buried his head farther into his pillow, hiding from the sun that shown through the window. As much as he wasn't enjoying the light, it loved him. His messy pitch-black hair glistened like obsidian in the sun rays, and his dark lashes casted shadows across his cheeks.

I waited for the same wave of panic to overtake me that had come yesterday morning, after the loss of my self-control in the elevator. It didn't come. Instead, a deep sense of satisfaction filled me, and I snuggled further into Sebastian's bed.

I had spent the whole of yesterday thinking I was about to get my heart torn apart like a little girl whose first crush didn't like her back. He wasn't supposed to return my feelings, but he had. And despite the list of reasons why we shouldn't have fallen into bed together, I couldn't bring myself to wish the night had ended differently.

Or the morning, as it were.

The glowing red lights on his bedside clock told me it was eleven, and I almost couldn't believe it. I hadn't gotten up this late since I was drafted to Seattle's farm team three years ago. Whether I was practicing, playing, or doing nothing that day, I always got up early.

But that was before I met the sex machine known as Sebastian Kingston. I could only be glad that we didn't have mandatory practice today. Still, a run couldn't hurt.

But someone had other plans.

"Are you leaving?" grumbled a muffled voice. Sebastian picked up his head, his hair stuck up in every possible direction, and was immediately blinded by the sun. He let out a squeak and slapped a hand over his eyes. "Dear God, what time is it?"

"It's eleven."

Like a mouse peeking out from his hidey-hole, Sebastian's fingers spread just enough to see through. I met a sliver of his eye through his fingers and fought a smile at his cuteness. I never expected a man as intimidating as him on the ice could be so sleep-rumpled and adorable.

"Seriously?" he asked in a disbelieving voice.

"Hey, I blame you for this. You're the one who kept us up all night. I should be on my morning run by now."

His hand dropped from his face and the full force of his gaze held me. A corner of his mouth lifted, his scar taunting me. "Are you saying you didn't enjoy it?"

I puckered my lips slyly and stretched under the comforter. My body thrummed pleasantly. "Irrelevant."

With the grace and fluidity of a predator on the prowl, he sat up, letting the sheets fall from his body and settle around his hips, revealing his taut, sculpted abdomen. I was suddenly wide awake, and judging by his thickening erection, so was he. "Oh, I'm so sorry that I ruined your cardio plans. Here, let me help you out get in a good workout."

He ripped the sheets off my body.

I managed to escape the bed as Sebastian hopped into the shower, giving my poor body a reprieve. My panties were in a pile, so I grabbed them and pulled them on, but our shirts were laying somewhere on the floor downstairs. Deciding to let the girls be free for a little while longer, I left my sports bra where it was on the carpet and grabbed the empty glasses that

Sebastian had brought up after our first-round last night.

A few minutes later, I was carefully balancing the refilled water glasses on my way up the stairs and into Sebastian's bedroom.

"It's like déjà vu all over again."

His sudden appearance, emerging from the en-suite bathroom just as I walked into his room, almost made me fumble the water glasses. *Shit.*

Sebastian chuckled at my jumpiness and fixed the towel around his waist, a smirk on his face. "Not that I'm complaining. This is definitely a sight that I will never get tired of."

I didn't get what he was talking about until I followed his gaze to my naked chest.

I snorted and set the glasses on the night-stand. "I'm never going to live that down, am I?"

Sebastian chuckled and walked toward me, still focused on my bare tits. "You have to admit, it was a great introduction. Although, I think I prefer this time."

"And why's that?"

"Because I can do this now." He reached out with both hands and cupped my tits.

Geez, you would think he would be used to them after having them in his mouth all last night. Rolling my eyes good-naturedly, I let him say hello to the girls. I mean, he hadn't seen them in over ten minutes. That must have been torture for him.

To be fair, I got what he meant because for the first time, I could give in to my desire to press my whole body against his freshly showered one.

I took a step forward, closing the last of the distance between us, and wrapped my arms around the back of his neck. My movements forced him to let go of my boobs, and his hands moved down my bare sides and settled on my ass. Using his new grip on me, he held me close.

I dug my hand into the base of his water-logged hair, stirring up the scent of his shampoo. Sandalwood. I hummed in delight and buried my nose into his neck.

"Oh, and you do, by the way," he mumbled into my hair.

"Huh?"

"You have the best ass in the league."

Our conversation from last night came back to me, and I snorted in disbelief, pushing off him a few inches so I could look into his gorgeous face. "Of course, I have the best ass. I'm a goaltender. I basically spend the entire game in a squat. I would demand a refund if it wasn't toned to hell and back."

"Maybe you should get a refund anyway. It is a little pale," he chirped and squeezed said ass.

"Hey. Rude. I'm Russian. Everything about me is pale. And all your coloring is artificial."

We both looked down at his chest, the water-color-like ink illuminated in the bright bedroom. I hadn't studied them last night, a little occupied with other things, but now that I wasn't avoiding looking at Sebastian in a locker room, I could get a good look at the designs.

Both of his arms, his chest, and his sides were covered in ink. The bold black lines and small designs reminded me of old-school sailor tattoos. But instead of solid, saturated colors filling in the patchwork images perfectly, a rainbow of colors floated around his skin, not staying within any lines, and melting into each other. Releasing one hand from around his neck, I ran my palm down his shoulder and over his colorful peck.

"You could always get your own color," Kingston suggested as I traced the image of a bird splashed with yellow and blue ink.

"Yeah? Gonna recommend me your artist?"

"Uhh..."

I looked up at him in question, and his red face made my eyebrows raise.

"Actually... *I'm* my artist. I designed all these," he said as if confessing his deepest, darkest secret. Maybe he was.

I jerked back, forcing his hands off me, and stepped away to get a full look at him, covered in beautiful art. "You—you draw?"

Sebastian shrugged tight shoulders. "Yeah. I do other things too. I like to paint and sculpt. I'm working on making my own plates right now, but simple sketching is my favorite medium. I've been doing it since I was a kid."

My mind was completely blown. Of all the hobbies I expect Sebastian Kingston to have, art was at the bottom of the list. Not that it was long; I kind of thought he lived and breathed only hockey. Lord knew I did.

"Well, you're incredibly talented. If I ever decide to get stabbed a million times, you'll be the person I talk to first."

Sebastian chuckled. "It's a date."

And just like that, he took a knife to my bubble.

I didn't know what my face looked like, but it couldn't have been pretty. Sebastian hardened until he was the immovable wall that had one of the highest shot percentages in the league.

"Or not." His voice was like gravel, and I fought a flinch.

"I—I..." I sighed and collapsed onto the edge of his bed. After a tense moment, Sebastian slowly joined me.

"Crap," I mumbled to myself, then, with a deep breath, pulled my shoulders back and met Sebastian's gaze dead on. "Look, I don't know what you want out of this, but I cannot be in a relationship right now. Not only have I just started my career and don't have time for one, but it cannot be with a teammate."

Sebastian's lips pressed into a thin line. "Right."

"That doesn't mean I don't like you. Because, unfortunately, I really do. But if we got into a relationship and somebody found out, it would fuck up our careers, Sebastian. Sure, there's not any rules about teammates dating, but what team would want that kind of drama? Hell, the Blizzards didn't want the drama of me just being a woman, and that was without any relationship mess. If anyone found out, one of us would be traded."

Sebastian nodded. "And it wouldn't be me."

I let out a tiny sigh in relief. He understood. "No, it wouldn't be."

"So, we keep this secret?"

"And light," I insisted. "We're not dating. We're not boyfriend and girlfriend. We're teammates and friends. Who's to say we can't hang out? I mean, I'm a lesbian, right? And you're my mentor."

"Hang out?"

I nodded and waited, my lungs frozen, as Sebastian worried his lower lip between his teeth.

"Okay, but I have one condition: no sleeping with other people."

"No problem," I agreed as fast as possible. Hell, I barely had time and energy for this.

Sebastian's eyes suddenly snapped wide. "Wait. What about Mason? He knows you're here right now."

I winced. "Crap. Yeah, I already told him about molesting you in the elevator." Sebastian snorted at that, and I smiled. "There's no way I can keep this from him. Or my brother."

"Can they keep a secret? I don't know your brother, but I've seen Mason's poker face. Yours is better."

I chuckled. Mason sure had everyone fooled with his innocent, I-have-nothing-to-hide face. "Mason can keep his mouth shut when it matters. And Drew would never say anything."

"Okay."

"Do you want to tell anybody? Maybe Jones?" I asked. Sebastian hung out with Jones more than anyone else on the team. They were best friends.

"Yeah. If that's okay with you."

"Of course. Just you, me, Mason, Drew, and Jones. Our little bubble."

Sebastian's face lost the last of its hardness. "Sounds perfect."

I stared in horror at Mason's Jeep, still parked in front of my house. Oh, fuck. What was I about to walk in on?

I considered taking the short walk back to Sebastian's, but even at one in the afternoon, the February air was too harsh to stay out in a moment longer.

So, tugging my coat tight, I steeled myself, walked up to the house, swung open the door, and stepped inside.

It was quiet. Suspiciously quiet. I didn't trust that.

With careful, doubtful steps, I moved through the foyer and into the living room. I immediately clocked the mess. Clothing was strewn across the couch and floor, looking like they were tossed to the side in a rush. Suspicions confirmed.

A loud bang came from the kitchen. With a squeak, I turned my back to the sound, not wanting to catch a glimpse of anything.

I heard a distinctly Drew-like curse, then nothing.

"Drew?" I called out tentatively.

"Riles?"

"Yeah. You decent?"

"Mostly."

"Oh, thank the lord," I breathed out and walked into the kitchen.

Drew, alone, was making sandwiches. He was also only wearing pajama pants and had some interesting marks across his chest. Ah-ha. Caught red-handed.

I couldn't help myself; I applauded and let out a long wolf whistle.

"Oh, don't even," he grumbled.

I pouted, but stopped, and hopped onto the kitchen counter to stare at him.

"That's not much better."

"Well, sucks to suck." I flipped him off.

He rolled his eyes and went back to slathering mayo on some bread. I gestured for him to make me one as well.

We sat in silence as Drew slapped together ingredients. Before I had gotten traded to the Blizzards, I hadn't seen him in person in months.

He was busy with work, and I was always training. Still, we always made time to talk. He would rant to me about his coworkers, and I would do the same. We were each other's rocks and had been since that disastrous plane crash.

I was fifteen, just starting to work toward my NHL dream, and Drew was nineteen and in college when our parents' plane went down. We were suddenly orphans, and the grief should have destroyed us. No one would have blamed us if it had, but Drew saved us.

He transferred from Harvard to NYU and raised his little sister for years. Everyone told him I would have been better off with a distant relative or in foster care, but he refused to listen. Barely out of childhood himself, he was determined to keep the last of our family together, and I was eternally grateful to him.

"So, Mason said you went to Sebastian Kingston's place to talk last night."

"Mason said that, huh? And where *is* Mason this fine afternoon?" I asked slyly then internally celebrated when Drew tried to deflect.

"You slept with Kingston," he accused.

"And you slept with Mason."

We stared each other down, willing the other to admit what we both already knew.

The glare-off only lasted a few seconds before Drew sighed heavily and slapped the last of the sandwiches together. He'd made enough to feed an army. I pilfered one and stuffed it in my mouth. "Riles, I hate to break it to you, but I think we're idiots."

"Speak for yourself," I said around a mouthful of turkey and rye. "You're the one moving across the county."

Drew took a neat bite of a sandwich, chewed, and swallow. "He told you about that, huh?"

"So, it's true?"

"I've already got an offer from a friend from NYU. I'm gonna take it."

I finished off the rest of my sandwich and stopped myself from grabbing another. If I let myself, I could eat the whole plate. "Well, you're not going to hear me complaining about that. I've missed my big brother."

A soft look overtook Drew's face. "I've missed you too, Riles."

"What about Mason? He was freaking out a little bit. Seemed to think you guys were doomed to end in a ball of flames. Did you get him to..." I gave his hickey-covered chest a pointed glance. "... calm down?"

Drew rubbed the corner of his eye with his middle finger. "We had a talk, and I reasoned with him."

"Right. And when that didn't work?"

"Then I called him a pussy and dared him to nut up."

I burst into laughter. Damn. That would be sure to give Mason the push he needed. If I had any doubts about Mason and Drew's compatibility, they were gone now. Then a sobering thought occurred to me. "Wait. Are you going back into the closet? Because Mason's only out to us and his family."

"Yeah. For now."

"And you're okay with that?"

Drew finished his sandwich and grabbed another. "I know what I'm getting into."

I watched him dubiously. Drew had come out the second he knew that he was gay. He'd never hidden his sexuality a day in his life, but I didn't question him. Drew wasn't impulsive. If he decided to do this, he had already made a pros-and-cons list and had chosen the best option.

"Speaking of. Do you know what you're getting into with Kingston?"

I waved away his concerns. "I like Sebastian. He's nice and hot." Drew nodded in agreement at that. "And we both know what our priorities are. We're not dating. We're just casually hanging out. In secret."

"Hanging out," he repeated in disbelief.

I smirked at him and wiggled my eyebrows. "Yep."

His nose scrunched. "Nasty, Riles."

"What's nasty?" Mason asked as he came sauntering into the kitchen, wearing only jeans and covered in the same marks as Drew. He immediately zeroed in on the stack of food and grabbed two sandwiches from the top of the pile.

"Nothing I want to talk about if I plan to get this sandwich down."

"Aww, come on. You were the one to give me the birds and the bees talk," I teased.

"Ughh. God, woman." Drew turned to Mason. "Do you want some water, babe?"

"Yes, please," Mason answered, and Drew was off to the fridge.

Aww, they were adorable. Mason must have read my mind because he stuck his tongue out at me. I just leaned back on the counter and waited.

It only took a second for him to clock my pantsuit—the same one I was wearing last night. And I did not doubt that my hair could use a brush.

His eyebrows shot up. *There we go. We both got laid last night.*

Then with a look to make sure Drew was distracted, Mason stuck his fist out. I bumped it in victory.

During the next game, Kingston and I were perfectly civil. As far as the team knew, we had gotten over that little antagonist bump and were now friends. We talked casually and amicably in the locker room as usual but made sure to stay a respectable distance apart and keep our eyes to ourselves. If anything, I looked at him less than I did before.

On the ice, however, we barely had to make an effort.

I skated by Sebastian on my way to the net and flashed a platonic smile at him. He returned it, but when I reached the net and glanced at him again, his face was back to its usual blankness.

I was a little put off by Kingston's particular brand of play. Sure, everyone was intense on the ice, they had to be, but Kingston took it to a whole new level. I didn't think I'd ever seen him smile during a game. Not even during the calm lulls. He was always too tuned into the action.

He was also the same during practice. The other guys worked hard during practices to improve their skills, but they also had fun—laughing and joking around as they shot at the goals and practiced their stick handling. Kingston just stood off to the side, watching over everybody and then bringing his a-game when it was his turn to go through the drills.

During our extra practice with Mason, he had shown a smile or two, he had even cracked a joke, but now there was nothing. The only time I'd seen him visibly enjoying himself on the ice was during the charity practice he brought me to.

As I watched him now, barely talking to anybody as both teams warmed up, I wondered if he wouldn't rather be anywhere else.

12

I sat out in the hallway, humming along to my music and nodding at teammates and stadium workers as they passed. I got a few weird looks at my mood, but most nodded back.

Today was the day. I felt amazing, the sun was shining, and I was playing at the Snow Globe Arena like I had every week for weeks now. Any worries I had floated away.

Usually at this time, I would be meditating, juggling, or concentrating on getting my head in the game. But today I woke up ready to dominate. The second I walked into the arena, I knew what was going to happen. I just needed one thing.

Tommy came jogging up the hallway just in time, his head on a swivel, searching. I jumped up, and he stopped in front of me. "Did you get it?"

He held out a plastic bag, and I looked inside to see an assortment of nail polish. I squealed and hugged him. "Thank you so much!"

He looked startled when I released him but smiled tentatively back at me. "No problem, Miss Warren. Is there anything else I can do for you?"

"Nope. That's it."

He wished me a good game and headed off. He was one of the arena workers, and I had asked him to go out to the nearest store and grab me some polish. I couldn't go myself because I didn't want to get mobbed. So I was eternally grateful to him for getting a great selection of colors. I had half a mind to dedicate this game to him.

I sorted through the bag as I made my way to the lounge area. By the time I made it, I had settled on the hot pink polish and was shaking it like a maniac.

The locker was half full and chaotic as usual. Guys were in their workout clothes as they lounged around, some in a light stretch, others taping their sticks.

"Whatcha got there, Warren?" Ethan Jones asked. He had seen me suddenly jump up out of my skin and excitedly wave down Tommy thirty minutes ago.

I held up the pink polish so he could get a good look, and his face turned incredulous.

"Nail polish. That's what you had the kid go get?"

"What? I've got to look fabulous, Jones. Not that you would know anything about that, but I could help you out. Want me to paint your nails after I do mine?"

He looked horrified, and the guys around him laughed. Beside him, Sebastian gave me a confused look, probably wondering why I thought it was a good time to paint my nails. I just smiled at him and took a seat in my cubby.

Not wasting time, I carefully applied the first coat to my nails then blew on them to dry. The guys all looked at me weirdly. I ignored them. The second coat went on smoothly, and just as I finished my last pinkie, a few more guys entered the locker room, Mason among them.

"Holy shit, Riles! Are you painting your nails?" he asked excitedly.

"Yep, you want in?"

He didn't hesitate and sat next to me, hands held at the ready. I forwent my topcoat and handed Mason the bag of nail polish. Like a homing missile, he found the neon green polish and handed it to me. It was the same color as his Jeep. Laughing at him under my breath, I shook up the bottle. Mason was the only person I knew who had a lucky color.

Not that he needed the luck; lately, he was so on fire that I was surprised the rink didn't melt under his skates. And it wasn't hard to guess why. Although Drew had been back in California for a week to get ready to move, their relationship was strong, and any second thoughts Mason had about hooking up with Drew were out the window.

"What the hell, Frey? You too?" Berg asked, looking like he wanted to slap the polish out of my hands with his half-taped stick.

"Yeah, I didn't think that was your color," Jones mocked, and another chuckle rolled through the room.

To be fair, Jones had a point. As much as it was his lucky color, it did not agree with his skin tone. However, I was not one to mock superstition, so I got to work.

"Don't underestimate the power of the polish, guys," Mason warned the guys as I was busy painting. Unlike on my nails, I only did a few fingers on each of Mason's hands.

Once I was done, he blew on them and then carefully drew out his phone. We posed for a selfie, showing off our nails. Mason posted it to his Instagram.

The guys ribbed us as we went about getting ready for the game. I kept the secret to myself anytime they questioned me. But Mason, like the dork he was, clasped his green hands together and intoned like a prayer, "Power of the polish."

"Power of the polish!" Jones screamed and attacked me. He was the closest to the net when the final buzzer sounded, and he lifted me off my skates in his bear hug. The team was seconds behind, and they bulldozed into the group hug, shouting "Power of the polish" into my ears.

When we eventually pulled apart, I was slightly dizzy. They had spun me around too much. Also, my eardrums may have ruptured.

Not having joined in the hug-pile, Sebastian skated up and steadied me with a hand on my arm. Once he was sure I wasn't going to tip over, he let me go and held up a puck.

"Congrats on your first shut out." His face was as blank as usual when he was on the ice, but I could have sworn I heard a smile in his voice.

I took the puck that would be joining my collection, which included the first puck I ever stopped, the first puck I let in, a puck from Rachel McCarthy, and a few others.

"Ms. Warren. We saw the pictures posted by Mason Frey before the game. Do you really think painting your nails in the locker room is appropriate?"

"Why wouldn't it be? Everyone has a routine before games."

"Yes, but you also painted Mason Frey's nails. Don't you think forcing your femininity onto your teammates is going to affect their game?"

"I wasn't forcing anything on anybody." I was getting tired of this guy and was one more stupid question away from losing my shit.

"Well, the team needs to be aggressive on the ice, and girly nail polish could diminish their confidence. You have a responsibility to keep your female activities to yourself to preserve the environment of the NHL."

"Excuse me?" I said, leaning forward. But before I could say anything else, Jones darted into the impromptu press conference taking place in the hallway. He paid the reporters no attention and came up to my side.

"Damn, Warren. I should have taken you up on your offer. Those nails are fierce. But I don't think that pink is for me." Blocking me from view, he steered me back into the players' lounge. The press tried to follow but were blocked by half the Blizzards' defensemen. Good luck getting through them. In other news, I was never leaving the lounge before the rest of the guys again, no matter how badly I needed to walk out the cramps in my thighs.

"How about orange?" I asked Jones.

"Philly orange? God no!"

"You're right. That's my bad. I can do Blizzards' blue and white."

"That's more like it."

"There you are, Warren! Are we going out to celebrate?" Henry Nicks asked, emerging from the kitchen area with a protein shake in hand.

"Oh, God no. I'm dead tired but have a drink in my honor."

"Will do." Nicks saluted me with his shake and wandered away. A second later, I heard, "Decker! You coming out tonight?"

Jones slung an arm around my shoulders. "Aw, you're not going to celebrate, Warren? What are you, an old woman?"

"Just not feeling a bar tonight."

"What about a night in? Some video games? A couple non-alcoholic beers?"

God that sounded perfect. Well, not the beers. But the rest? "I'm down for that."

"Great, come on." With the arm over me, he dragged me into the locker room. He looked around and immediately found his target. "Oi, Kingston. Video games tonight at your place? You, me, and Warren? We need a Mortal Kombat rematch. I'm pretty sure you cheated last time."

Sebastian shrugged. "I didn't cheat. You just suck, but sure. Let's make a night of it. You coming too, Frey?"

Mason's head perked up from his locker. "Old-school Mortal Kombat? You couldn't keep me away if you tried."

"Eat it, Frey!" Jones yelled.

"Don't get cocky, bitch! I'm on your ass," Mason shot back, and his character kicked Jones' in the face.

We hadn't even been in Sebastian's brownstone for an hour, and the boys were already ready to throw controls and drop metaphoric gloves. It was a good thing they were separated on either side of the sectional.

I'd played a couple rounds but mostly left them to themselves, content to lay on Sebastian's soft, black couch and watch their back-and-forth like a tennis match. But now I needed a new drink. Where was...

"Here you go," Sebastian said.

"Thank you." I grabbed the wine cooler he handed me and took a sip as he dropped off fresh beers to Mason and Jones.

Watermelon-flavored deliciousness flooded my tongue, and I was glad I dropped by my house to grab some palatable alcohol. Usually, I would have stopped at one. I couldn't afford all the sugar, but the season was almost over. So I was on my second drink, with no intention of stopping soon. It seemed the boys were letting themselves go too. They had broken out the high-carb, alcoholic beer like true rebels.

"Fuck," Jones cursed suddenly and took an angry sip from his bottle, glaring at Mason. "Tiebreaker, Frey. Winner takes all."

With a harsh snort, Kingston settled onto the large couch beside me. "Don't you get tired of always losing, Jones?"

"Don't get comfy, King. After I get done wiping the floor with Frey here, I'm coming after you."

"Big words," I said.

"I can back it up."

Oh. Cocky. "You know what? Hundred bucks on Mason."

"Hell yeah!" I slapped the hand Mason raised.

"Aw, man. I guess I'm stuck with Ethan," Sebastian said, calling my bet.

"Now we've got some stakes. Let's do this!" Jones took one last sip of beer then faced the screen with renewed determination.

As a voice announced the next fight on the screen, I popped off the couch, but I didn't go far. It took a few slaps to Sebastian's thighs for him to understand what I wanted. But with a raised eyebrow, he spread his legs, and I took my spot between them. His arm went around my waist, and I leaned back into his chest to watch the virtual battle.

He hummed, his chest vibrating, and took a pull from his beer.

After a lot of cursing from Mason and Jones and cheers from me and Sebastian, Mason came out with the W.

"Guess who owes me a hundred buck." I wiggled against Sebastian.

"Do you want cash? Or can I pay you off a different way?" He growled into my ear, sending shivers through me. I was just about to reach up and pull him to my mouth when...

"Wait. You guys are together?" Jones asked.

I furrowed my eyebrows. "I thought you knew."

"I hadn't told him yet," Sebastian rumbled behind me.

"Since when has this been going on?" Jones asked then turned to Mason. "Did you know about this?"

Mason shrugged. "Yeah"

Jones turned back to me. "But... I thought you were..."

"Bisexual," I filled in.

Jones' mouth snapped shut, and he just stared at us, expression blank and controller forgotten in his hand. Dear God, we'd killed him.

"It's pretty new," I told Jones, hoping to bring him back to life.

"I knew it," he shouted abruptly, and I jumped in Sebastian's arms. He pointed over me at Sebastian. "I knew you were staring at her ass."

"What?" I asked.

"He was staring at your ass while you were on the treadmill a couple days ago. I caught him, but he convinced me that I was hallucinating the whole thing. I was seriously questioning my eyesight for a minute."

"Nah, you're all good," Mason said, obviously enjoying this moment. "He's always staring at her."

I looked up in question.

Sebastian met my eyes and shrugged.

"Way to be subtle, dude," I hissed and elbowed him in the side.

"Not like you're any better, Riles," Mason said.

I whipped my head toward Mason and stabbed my finger at him. "That's defamation. Or libel. Or whatever."

He smirked at me from his safe position on the couch.

Oh, it was on.

I pushed up off the couch … and was immediately yanked back down by Sebastian. "You can't kill him yet," he said. "I have to go kick his virtual ass and claim my title as champion."

I pouted but let him wiggle out from under me.

He took over Jones' spot, and Jones joined me on the couch. I immediately perked up and reached for my bag on the floor. Digging around, I pulled out two bottles of nail polish. "You ready, Jones?"

He sputtered and started to protest. "Wait. I was just kid—"

"Ah, ah, ah. I brought blue and white as requested. There's no backing out now."

He glared at me for a moment, but when I didn't give in to his captaincy presence, he relented.

"Fine but make them look good." He thrusted his hands toward me, turning to watch the television like he couldn't bear witness to the defiling of his precious nails.

I gave the bottles a quick shake then started coating his nails in the first layer of light blue.

"I assume you guys are keeping this, whatever it is, from the press?"

"You assume correctly. Secret and very casual. If it ever came out, our careers would be done, and I'm not ready to give up hockey. I'm just getting started and hopefully have a lot of time left in the game. And Sebastian has more than a few good seasons left in him, so this is staying casual. It has to."

Jones hummed, and I looked up in time to see his eyes flicker toward Sebastian, a weird expression on his face. "Right. Who would want to give up their career in the NHL?"

"Exactly."

I finished the second coat of blue then fished out a brush from the bag. The nail art brush was precise and steady as I carefully drew snowflakes on Jones's middle fingers as accents. When I was finished, I brushed on a quick topcoat and sat back to admire my work.

"Not bad, Warren. I'm keeping these for as long as possible. And when we crush our next game, that little reporter bastard will eat his words."

"Hell yeah!"

"Riles, I kicked your boytoy's ass. You up next?" Mason asked.

"Thanks, but I get my ass kicked enough by you without an audience. I'm good."

Ethan clapped. "Rematch time."

"Don't mess up your nails. They're still wet," I yelped as he sprang from the couch and took the controller from Sebastian. He better not fuck up my masterpieces.

"I'm never playing Frey again," Sebastian grumbled and slumped beside me.

"Aw. Don't feel too bad. Mason's a video game nerd. He's been playing Mortal Kombat since he was six. Here, do you want me to do your nails?

It always cheers me up," I teased, fully expecting him to refuse.

But he shrugged and held out his hands. "Sure. Why not?"

I did the same design on Sebastian that I did to Ethan but inverted the colors. When I was done, Sebastian had white nails sprinkled with dainty blue snowflakes.

13

*W*arren, you dumb bitch, what the hell are you doing? I thought harshly as I carefully finished applying my dark red lipstick. With a smack of my lips, I stepped back to check my makeup. It was perfect.

And entirely wrong!

"Why does this feel like a date?" I asked my reflection. Her exasperated face called me an idiot.

Sebastian and I had been "hanging out" for about three weeks now, and it was going well. Our work schedule was hectic, but between road trips, games, and practices, we managed to meet up once a week at his place. We were keeping it casual as we promised. I'd gone to another charity practice with him and had even let him drag me to a bar with the whole team once. As far as the team, outside of Mason and Jones, was concerned, we were just mentor and mentee.

But now I was dressing up in my favorite little black dress and fuck-me Louboutins, and I couldn't deny this was veering into date territory. Unfortunately, that wasn't as horrendous an idea as it was months ago.

I was going over to Sebastian's house to cook him dinner because of a dare. I blamed Mason; he was the one who disparaged my cooking skills again, causing Sebastian to challenge me. Not one to ignore a thrown-down gauntlet, I accepted and challenged Sebastian in turn. He would be whipping up a dessert.

This was flirting with the boundaries we'd set, and I should have canceled. But when my phone dinged just as someone knocked on my front door, I couldn't contain the stutter of my heart. Sebastian was here!

I fluffed my freshly curled hair, grabbed my purse, scampered down the stairs in my pumps, opened the door, and almost doubled over as oxygen fled my lungs in a rush. I wasn't the only one who was putting effort into tonight, it seemed, and I couldn't be happier about that, because Sebastian looked edible. His wine-red shirt was rolled up to reveal his inked forearms and tucked into his black slacks, outlining the steep cut of his waist. The first couple buttons of his shirts were undone, gaping across his chest, and I wanted to lean forward and leave a lipstick print on him. It would have been the perfect addition because my lips and his shirt were the same color.

"We match," I said with a chuckle once I got my breath back.

Sebastian wasn't listening. Instead, he was transfixed on my dress as he stepped into my house. I backed up as he prowled forward, and the door slammed shut behind him.

"What? Do you like?" I asked saucily and twirled on the balls of my heels. My A-line dress fluttered around me gracefully, and I knew the second he saw the back because a growl left him. The dress was mostly conservative, not too short, and with sleeves that ended at my wrist. But what modesty it projected in the front was ruined the second I turned around, showing my fully bare back.

Sebastian caught me mid-twirl, and I stumbled to a stop in his arms.

"You look gorgeous," he breathed out, and his eyes flicked to my lips.

Oh, no, sir.

I pressed a finger to his mouth the second he leaned forward and tsked, "Lipstick."

With a playful pout in his eyes, he wrapped his tongue around my finger. Oh, I remembered that tongue. I liked that tongue. Maybe the ruin of my lipstick would be worth it.

The hands that had caught me by the waist started to slide, and I arched into Sebastian as they caressed the exposed expanse of my back. A soft moan escaped me, and Sebastian smiled against my finger.

"You ready to get out of here?" Sebastian asked.

"Yep. I'm good to g—"

"Babe, have you seen my hoodie?" Mason asked as he thudded down the stairs, wearing plaid boxers and nothing else. As he reached the last step, he saw me and Sebastian entangled in the foyer and stopped short.

Sebastian let me go.

"Uh. Hi." Mason grinned awkwardly and rubbed his neck, bringing attention to the hickey there and the ones scattered across his chest.

"What the hell?" Kingston looked between us, face hard. "Why is he half naked in your house?"

"Dude, no," I vehemently denied his implication. My disgusted face matched perfectly with Mason's. I thought I had already assured him that Mason and I were not like that.

Sebastian jabbed a finger at Mason. "What am I supposed to think, Riley? You're always hanging off him. And now he's at your house, half-naked."

Mason jumped in. "I'm like her brother."

"Then who's giving you hickeys?"

I clamped my mouth shut. It was up to Mason if he wanted to come out to Sebastian, and I wasn't going to pressure him. If he didn't want to, I would find a way to defuse Sebastian.

But, before Mason could choose, the decision was made for him.

"What, babe?" Drew asked as he came around the corner from the kitchen. I hadn't realized he was in there. Unfortunately, he was only wearing sweatpants, his chest covered in hickeys identical to Mason's. These boys really had the worst timing

We all froze. Sebastian's face turned red, his face the epitome of "oh." I snorted then quickly slapped a hand over my mouth. Looked like the cat was out of the bag.

"Shit," Drew's eyes flickered frantically between us all, obviously looking for a way to explain this situation. "I was just—"

I waved him off. It was too late now, and Sebastian wasn't stupid.

"It's okay, babe." Mason comforted Drew, then, visibly steeling himself, turned to Sebastian. "We good?"

"Yeah. Sorry," Sebastian mumbled sheepishly.

I cleared my throat. "Sebastian, this is my brother, Drew Warren. Drew, this is Sebastian Kingston."

Sebastian stepped forward and thrust out his hand, his nails still spotted with the remains of white polish. "Nice to meet you, man."

Drew shook it and smiled wryly. "You too."

"Well, this has been interesting, but I think we're going to head out. See you guys later." I gave the boys a little wave then quickly steered Sebastian out the door. The second it shut behind us, laughter tore from me.

Hours later, I collapsed onto the comfortable sectional, Sebastian following suit beside me. We just laid there for a minute, panting.

"I can't tell what was better—the meal or the dessert."

I snorted and shook my head at Sebastian's silly grin. "Well, it was definitely the dessert." I paused. "I mean, those cupcakes you made were delicious. Lemon is my favorite. And who would have thought you were a baker? Maybe I should get you an apron. I could even put your name and team number on it."

"Damnit, Warren!"

"Oh, did you mean the sexual dessert?" I reached out and ran my nails down his abs innocently. "I guess that was okay too."

A laugh huffed out of Sebastian as he sat up on the sofa and crossed his legs under him. I stayed on my back in front of him, splayed out like a buffet. He poked me in the side, and I wiggled my nude body away from him, giggling.

"Who would have thought I would be getting chirped more in the bedroom than I do on the ice," he said wryly.

I cheesed so hard up at him that my cheeks started to hurt. "But you make it so easy."

"Or you're just a smartass." His head cocked to the side. "A smartass who looks like a sexed-up Joker."

"What?"

He swiped his finger over my chin, and when he pulled it back to show me, it was streaked with red. "I ended up ruining your lipstick after all."

Aw, damn. My mascara was probably smeared around my eyes as well. But thankfully, I came prepared.

"Could you grab my purse right there?"

While Sebastian reached out and grabbed the bag from the edge of the couch, I finally sat up, my sex-sore muscles stretching pleasantly.

"Thank you." I dug out the makeup wipe from the purse and scrubbed my face. "Better?" I posed for Sebastian with another huge smile.

"Almost." He took the wipe from me, wrapped it around his finger, then rubbed gently around my eyes. When he was done, he pinched my chin and tilted my head from side to side. "There's the woman I know."

"What? You didn't like my makeup?"

His thumb swiped my cheek, his eyes tracing my face. "You looked beautiful tonight, Riley. That dress, like the woman inside it, was breathtaking."

My cheeks heated under his thumb. "Thank you. I don't always dress up, but I figured you'd like it. I think it's the first time you've seen me out of athleisure or pantsuits."

"Riley, trust me when I say it doesn't matter what you wear, I can never keep my eyes off you."

"Even when I'm in full pads?" I asked, amazed at the sincerity in his voice.

"Oh, especially then. Did you know I stare at you when you take water breaks? I watch when you take off your mask. There's sweat running down your face, and your hair is coming out of your braids. You look like a fucking mess…" He groaned, his eyes far away before he snapped back to reality. "I have to force myself to look away before I pop a boner on the ice."

"W-what?"

"And when we get into the locker room, you immediately take off your sweater and unsnap your upper pads. Uh, God."

"I'm still fully clothed then!" I've never seen any of my other teammates, even the ones who were attracted to me, look at me with lust when I was freshly covered in sweat. God, Kingston was a freak. I couldn't stop the incredulous smile on my face.

"It doesn't matter. You look like a warrior ready to face anyone who challenges you, gorgeous and deadly. It's like staring at a Valkyrie. I've never seen anything like it or met anyone like you. You drive me insane but, at the same time, are the only thing that's keeping me sane."

I stared at him, at a complete loss, as his words bounced around my insides like pinballs, tearing up my heart and stirring my stomach.

Flat on my back in his bed, I spread my arm to Sebastian in invitation. Immediately, he flopped lengthwise onto me and rested his head on my sternum. I opened my legs, his stomach slotting between them, and buried my hand into his damp, silky hair.

Sebastian let out a soft sound as my nails scratched across his skull, and he snuggled in closer to me.

"Whatever you do, please don't stop." His voice was drifting.

"Are you falling asleep on me?" I asked, not stopping.

"Yeah. We have a big game in a couple days. You're going to need to catch a few hours yourself if you have a hope of stopping Glass."

A savage smile that Sebastian couldn't see plastered across my face. "He has one of the hardest slapshots in the game. Did you know that he broke a hundred miles per hour a few months ago? It was only in practice, but it's still incredible. During games, his rockets are consistently in the high nineties. Add in that little deke he does—which is kind of like the awesome one you've pulled against me a dozen times now—and he's borderline impossible to stop. Hell, he's on his way to catching up with your shooting percentage. I can't wait to go toe to toe with him."

With a little grunt, Sebastian squirmed under my hands, and I realized that I had gripped his hair tight in my excitement. Whoops. I let go and smoothed down the disturbed strands in apology.

He settled again and sighed against me, the puff of air leaving goosebumps in its wake. "Is that why you love hockey so much? The challenge?"

"Well, yeah. What's the point of doing anything if you're not going to be the best? And the only way to do that is to play against people better and stronger than you."

"Is that why you never switched to women's hockey?"

"I guess. At first, it was because of Mason. He was my only friend, on and off our team. A lot of the other kids thought I was a little too energetic, but Mason didn't mind. So I followed him around like a baby duck for a while. As we got older, and the girls started separating from the guys, I fought to stay with them and Mason. Of course, most coaches didn't want me on their teams, even after I proved myself better than the other boys. That's when having two lawyers as parents came in handy." I chuckled.

Sebastian's head popped up, a single eyebrow raised. "Did they sue anybody?"

"No, no, no. They never had to go that far, but I'm sure they threatened more than a couple poor coaches. Though I didn't fully understand what they did for me until after they died, and Mason, Drew, and I had to practically fistfight my junior coach to let me on the team."

He folded his hand on my sternum and rested his chin on them, gazing at me through his thick lashes. "Did you ever want to quit hockey altogether?"

"I did once. After my parents died. I barely wanted to move from my bed, let alone go to fucking hockey practice. I didn't give a shit anymore, you know?"

He nodded at my rhetorical question. "What brought you back?"

I smiled. "Mason. My brother tried to help at first, but he had so many other things that he was taking care of at the time. He had bills, funeral arrangements, and college. For the first month after the funeral, before Drew and I got the hang of things, I hardly got out of bed. And Drew was so swamped with everything, while trying to cope with his feelings, that he just barely remembered to feed us every day. So, when I started to show signs of legitimate depression, Mason broke into my room and dragged me to a rink. We skated for hours. It was like magic—I finally remembered why I loved hockey so much and, weirdly, being on the ice helped me connect to my parents."

"Were they into hockey?"

"Oh God, yeah. My parents dragged me and Drew to games at the Snow Globe all the time. It was our family time. My parents were constantly busy with work, but they always tried to make time for a good hockey game. The arena became our home away from home. Hell, we did most of our homework in stadium seats. I think that's what made Drew hate hockey a little, but I fell in love. Those were the happiest days of my life. Your parents own a rink, right? You must have lived on that ice."

Sebastian heaved out a sigh and rolled off me. He landed on his side and flipped to face me. He tucked an arm under his head and chewed his lip.

"What? What did I say?" I asked, searching his face for the source of the abrupt mood shift.

With visible effort, Sebastian spoke. "My mother was a figure skater, and my father was a hockey player. They were high school sweethearts, and when they graduated, they decided to open a rink. So, the second I was able to walk, I was in skates. Then I started baby hockey, and we all discovered something. I was a prodigy. I picked up a hockey stick for the first time and could suddenly handle it like someone ten years older than me. Suddenly, my whole life was clearly spread out before me. I was destined for the big show. It was inevitable that I would end up in the NHL."

I was flabbergasted. I knew Sebastian was good, but I had never heard that he was an actual prodigy. It made total sense. Still... "Even a prodigy has to put in work on the ice. You can't succeed on just natural skill alone."

"True. My dad hired my first private coach when I was five. It was a stretch for his wallet, but it was worth it. I'm a quick study. Not only was I naturally good, but I improved fast. I spent all my free time practicing until doing drills was like watching cartoons for other kids. Hockey became more like second nature to me than anything else."

"What about your friends?" I could picture a little Sebastian doing drills on an empty rink. My heart ached for him.

"Even they only wanted to hang out on the ice. Eventually, like your brother going to the arena all the time, you get a little tired of it. I mean, I don't hate hockey, obviously. I wouldn't be here if I did. But I don't think I love it as much as you do. I don't think anyone does, to be honest."

14

*W*e were in the second period of our game against the Philly Tigers and were up 2-1. Lesso had snuck a puck past me at the end of the first, but I'd buckled down since then and became a wall.

I was impressing even myself. The Tigers were one of the top teams in our division and were pretty much guaranteed to go to the play-offs this year.

The Blizzards, however, had no chance of playing for the cup this playoff season. Lukin and I were still on goalie rotation and two of our best defensemen were out as well. To say that we were struggling defensively would be a severe understatement.

Still, my record was decent. Of the sixteen games I'd played since I got traded, we'd won thirteen and lost three—a more than passable record. Unfortunately, the same couldn't be said for my co-goalie, Lukin.

Of the nineteen games he played, we had won twelve and lost seven. While that certainly wasn't the best, it wasn't the worst that a rookie goalie has done in the league. What was worse was his attitude.

At first, Lukin was just cocky and a bit of an asshole. But, even as I won more games and he hit a losing streak, his attitude never changed. It was almost like he didn't see that he was doing badly. He never stayed after practice or put in more effort than what was required, and he went out with the other rookies every other night.

Even now, decked out in full goalie gear on the bench, he wasn't watching the game. He was totally zoned out, just barely aware enough to open the gate for our teammates as they stepped in and out. I wanted to go over there and smack him. The season was almost over, and he didn't have many chances left to prove himself. Considering all the work everyone else put in, including myself, his carefree attitude was insulting.

The whistle blew, and everyone switched shifts.

Taking advantage of the break, I shook off my glove, gripped my mask, and pulled it off. Hair stuck to my forehead, and sweat rolled down my temples. Grabbing my water bottle from the back of the net, I absentmindedly scanned the rink and found myself locking eyes with Kingston on the other end of the ice. I froze, water bottle held ready a foot from my face.

Suddenly, I didn't feel like a sweaty mess. With Sebastian's attention on me, I was Jessica fucking Rabbit. Looking off to the side, I elongated my neck, showing off my good side, and shot a stream of ice water into my mouth.

I caught it all, and when I turned back to Sebastian, my cheeks hurt from the amount of liquid they were holding. The slight pain was worth it, though, when I saw the tiny twitch of his mouth. Ha! Number of times Sebastian Kingston had smiled during a game: 1.

Everyone settled into position. I forced the water down, replaced my mask, and crouched in my crease.

The puck dropped. Charlie Glass, the Tigers' star forward with the wicked slapshot, came up with it then was off. His team managed to hold off our offense long enough for him to dash across the ice, heading straight for me, Ethan Jones on his tail. Jones wouldn't get to him fast enough. I shivered in anticipation and inched out of the net as he got closer, ready.

I rocked on my skate, tracking his movements. He got closer and jerked back and forth, trying to throw me off. I followed every twitch like a hypnotized cobra. His right skate came off the ice. He was going to go left. No. Right! I moved to intercept, but instead of his skate coming back down, the other one jerked, followed by his whole body.

Oh, shit.

There was no way to stop him or for me to get out of the way. I braced, and he impacted with all the force of a two-hundred-pound man skating over twenty miles per hour. We tangled and went down.

The ice under me, and the hockey player above me, stole my breath.

Ouch.

Thankfully, my head didn't bounce off the ice and the rest of me also felt unbroken. Immediately, Glass pushed himself up onto his feet and held out his hand. I could see an apology forming on his pained face as I reached up to accept his help. But before I could grab it, the hand, and Glass, were taken away by a blue-and-white blur.

In horror, I watched as Glass was forced into a shoving and shouting match by Sebastian Kingston.

Shit.

I ripped my mask off and got my feet under me, not even noticing Jones was beside me until he stopped my instant stumble. I didn't let my unsteadiness deter me from my goal though and waded into the pile of players that was forming by the boards. The Tigers had come to Glass' defense, and the Blizzards backed up their assistant captain. The linesmen were trying to break it up but to no avail. It made for a dense dog pile that I had to work through to get to my idiot.

I pushed past players, both my teammates and opponents, as I forced my way into the group, getting more pissed off as they held up their hands when they saw who I was and let me through. Right. Don't touch the girl goalie. Hell, don't touch a goalie at all.

It was an important rule in hockey—you fuck with someone's goalie, you're going to get slammed into the boards. And if you fuck with the only female player on the team, a bunch of overprotective guys will materialize out of thin air to beat the shit out of you. No one in their right minds would purposefully mess with a female goalie. Sure, hockey players weren't the smartest beings on the planet, but we weren't complete morons.

Well, maybe a couple were.

Case in point? The idiot I was sleeping with.

I made it to the center of the crowd. Kingston had Glass pinned up against the plexiglass with an unbreakable grip on his sweater. Glass had a similar hold on Kingston, but with a lot less anger.

"Take off your fucking gloves, Glass," Kingston shouted into his face. The expression on Kingston's face startled me for a second. I knew that he never smiled on the ice, but I hadn't realized that he never got mad on the ice either.

Even when he got into fights, he was famous for being ruthless and unemotional. He was "The King" after all. The competitive nature of the game always caused people's emotions to rise but never Kingston's. At least not until today. I didn't think I'd ever seen him this pissed, in person or on game tape. His teeth were bared, and spit was flying from his mouth with every shout.

I only paused for a millisecond before I got in there to break this bullshit up. I shoved my arms between theirs and pushed against their padded chests. "That's enough, Kingston. It was an accident."

They barely looked at me. I pushed again, knowing I wouldn't move them an inch; Glass was already against a wall, and Kingston was pushing against him with all his body weight and anger.

I caught Sebastian by the strap of his helmet, forced his head to turn toward me, and growled, "It was an accident. Let him go, Sebastian."

I held his fiery gaze. We were in a mental, and slightly physical, arm-wrestling match. I raised my eyebrows at him in challenge, not flinching.

Kingston held.

I held.

Kingston's grip loosened from Glass, and he let me push him a few inches away. I got in between them and faced Glass.

"Sorry," I said to Glass, a smile tight on my face.

His gaze flicked over my shoulder to Kingston for a second before returning to me. "No, I'm sorry."

I stopped him before he could go on. "It was an accident, Glass. I saw you trip, and I couldn't move out of the way fast enough. Sorry about my teammates. They get a little overprotective."

A smile flickered over his face. "I get it. If someone ran into my daughter, I would be all over them." His eyes widened and he quickly backtracked, hands held up as if I was about to attack him myself. "Not that you're fragile and need protecting. You're a hockey player who can handle herself."

My smile turned genuine at his babbling, and an ounce of anger drained from me. He was cute. Although his reference to Kingston as my father figure was a little off-putting.

Glass and I apologized to each other one more time. Thankfully, he didn't point out that Kingston didn't say sorry for overreacting and returned to his bench. His team followed him, and the scuffle was over.

I didn't look at Kingston as he was thrown into the sin bin by an irate linesman.

"Good game, guys," Coach said. "Frey, Garza, nice teamwork. Berg, you were a wall. Even I wouldn't have wanted to go against you in my prime." Coach's voice hardened a little. "Kingston, you need to get yourself together. It's your job to set an example for this team."

After the Kingston and Glass scuffle, it took me a while to settle down and get back into the groove of the game. The Tigers overtook us almost immediately, but after the break, I came back and stood firm in the third, not letting another puck past me.

Although, I don't think anyone noticed how off I was after the fight. Not with how erratic

Kingston was playing. He was one of the most consistent and emotionless players in the league, but I wouldn't have been surprised if he broke the record for the number of errors in a single hockey game tonight. He missed easy shots, and more than a couple pucks escaped from underneath the blade of his stick. They were rookie mistakes that Kingston hadn't even made in his first year. Thank God everyone else was on fire. It saved me and Kingston from dragging the team down.

Hansson didn't shout at Kingston like he did when the younger player fucked up. There was no need to. Kingston was fully aware of his fuck ups. Well, at least some of his fuck ups.

For the millionth time in the past forty-five minutes, Sebastian shot me a tight look, and I almost snorted like an angry bull. He had some nerve being mad at me for forcing him to back down from Glass. I was mad at him!

Unfortunately, I didn't think he knew why I was so mad. And that made him even more irritated. He was sitting in his locker, not saying a word. I doubted he even could, with how hard his teeth were fused together.

Coach finished his talk and sent us off. I passed Kingston on my way to the showers, feeling his eyes boring into the side of my face

I didn't have time for him right now. I had something else I needed to deal with.

"That was a rough collision, Riley. Are you okay?"

"I'm perfectly fine. I've gotten more bruises from falling off a swing set."

Maybe I should be grateful for Sebastian's drama on the ice. It took away some of the attention from me. I didn't have nearly as many reporters surrounding me as I usually did. They were busy questioning Sebastian about his behavior and getting few satisfying answers.

Good luck with that, guys.

He had returned to his usual stoicism and was mainly giving monosyllabic answers.

I, on the other hand, didn't have that luxury.

"I saw that you didn't try to throw a punch. In fact, you helped break it up. Do you think that the inclusion of women into hockey will change the spirit of the game?"

"What do you mean?" I asked, already knowing. At my forced innocent voice, Sebastian looked over from his own horde of reporters.

"Fighting is one of the draws of hockey. It's why men's hockey is more popular than women's. People love a good fight, but the more women that join the league, the less violent it's going to get. Do you think the inclusion of women will be the downfall of hockey as we know it?"

Sebastian's eyebrows rose at the blatant sexism in that question.

I didn't think I had ever been asked that so bluntly in person. Online? Sure. People are usually braver from behind a screen. But this guy just let it all out right in my face. It was kind of impressive—in a fucked up, raised-by-wolves kind of way.

Apparently, Lukin agreed with the guy because he let out a haughty chuckle from his spot a few yards away from me.

"Well, fighting in the NHL has been decreasing for years. It's just not efficient. This is, ultimately, a game. The goal is to get a puck in a net, not to punch someone in the face. That's what professional fighting is for. Also, I broke apart the fight because it was pointless. Glass ran into me by accident, regardless of what it may have looked like. I understand that teams have to avenge their goalies, but it wasn't interference this time. Hell, if he had done it on purpose, I would have tried to get a piece of him myself. I'm fully capable, just like every other woman, of taking care of myself. I know what I can do, and I know my limits."

As I finished with my mini rant, a look of understanding crossed Sebastian's face.

Ah, he got it.

We made brief eye contact, anger visibly already draining from him, before the next questions took our separate attentions.

15

"*K*eep quiet," a voice breathed into my ear, and I was towed into an empty room by a firm grip on my upper arm.

Behind me, the door slammed shut, shrouding us in complete darkness.

"Jesus Christ, Sebastian. Don't be so creepy." I hit the switch, and light bathed Sebastian and the room I used to meditate in before games.

"Sorry. I just couldn't let you go before I got to talk to you." His hand tensed absently, and a dull pain rolled through my arm.

"Okay, but you *do* actually have to let me go because I landed on my arm when Glass ran me over and that hurts."

Sebastian's hand jerked back like he had touched a hot stovetop. "Jesus. I'm sorry. Are you okay?" He squinted at my bicep as if trying to see through my jacket and furrowed his brow. "How bad is it?"

I stepped back and crossed my arms, ignoring the intense throbbing. "Seriously, Kingston?"

He flinched guiltily.

"Look, I'm not really in the mood to give another guy a lesson on feminism in sports right now. Could we maybe pick this up later?"

"No, no, wait." His voice, like his beautiful grey eyes, turned pleading. "You're right."

I eyed him warily. "I haven't even said anything. What am I right about?"

"Everything. Whenever you're going to say, you're right. I messed up. You're right. I shouldn't have done that. You're right. I overreacted. You're right. You can take care of yourself. You're right. The only thing I did was give it to press more ammo against you. You're right. This isn't a part of our agreement. You're right. You're right about everything, and I'm so sorry."

My arms dropped from my chest.

"I'm not going to argue with you here, Riley. I know this is my fault."

I sighed and walked to the far end of the room. Then back. Then again. "No. It's not all your fault. It's not your fault that you don't always treat me like Warren instead of Riley on the ice. It's not your fault because I don't always treat you like Kingston on the ice. I'm not supposed to flirt with you on the ice or make you smile mid-game. So if you got confused, that's on me. I can't treat you like a boyfriend, no matter how mu—"

I came to a screeching halt on my sixth lap across the room, staring at the wall in horror. *Damnit, Warren.*

My only hope was that Sebastian hadn't heard me. I almost snorted. Fat chance.

Proving me right, Sebastian grabbed me again, this time by the wrist, and tugged me around to face him. I turned willingly but kept my eyes down, staring at his bespoke soot-colored jacket. I wanted to run my palms down the fine fabric. I didn't. Gently, Sebastian placed the flat of his free index finger under my chin and guided my face up until I met his searching eyes.

"What did you just say?"

Silently, I begged him to drop it. To let me off the hook.

He refused to let me go. Grey eyes grew darker with hope as my lips stayed firmly sealed. He caressed my chin, his finger grazing the scar that I got the last time I let someone distract me on the ice. *Damn this man.*

I gave in. "You know what I just said."

That rare, perfect smile broke across his face. I couldn't help but stare, drawn in by the light that seemed to shine from his every pore.

"You want to be my girlfriend."

I rolled my eyes, but a smile tugged at my lips. I couldn't help it; his childlike giddiness was contagious. I melted.

"Can I tell you something, Riley?"

"Could I stop you if I tried?"

The lines on his temples crinkled, and the scar on his lip danced. His hand on my wrist slid down, and his huge palm engulfed mine. Our calluses rubbed together. I shivered and squeezed our entangled fingers.

With the hand on my chin, Sebastian pulled me closer. If I wasn't already wearing heels, I would have been on my tiptoes.

His breath brushed across my lips. "Do you want to be my girlfriend, Riley Warren?"

Yes. Yes. Yes.

"No," I said and slipped my hand from his.

He let me go, not looking surprised in the least. Only disappointed.

Well, that makes two of us. But...

"We've had this conversation. We can't do that. Hell, we shouldn't be doing whatever it is we're doing right now. Look what you just did on the ice! What bullshit would you, or would I, pull if we were actually dating?"

"I don't know. Want to find out?"

I growled and banged my head into the nearest solid surface—his chest. *Thud, thud, thud.*

Even when I was done taking my frustration out on Sebastian's pecks, and my brain pounded in protest, I couldn't bring myself to back away. I collapsed against him. His hands went to my waist and stroked down my sides.

"Hey, hey, hey," he murmured into my hair. "Just think about it. I'm not asking you to come out or anything. I know we have to keep this a secret, but maybe we can be secretly dating instead of secretly 'hanging out.' I have legitimate feelings. And I know you do too. We could be so good together. Just think about it. Okay?"

"Sebastian," I whined to his chest, fighting the urge to shout "yes!" His speech was so tempting. And he was right; we *would* be so good together. But it wasn't that easy, was it?

"No, no. Don't answer now. Take a day or two. I'm sure you need to hit the gym to think or talk it over with your brother or Mason. So I'm going to leave before you can turn me down." He let me go and backed up to the door, hands held up as if to ward off any of my protests. "Get back to me tomorrow."

He pushed open the door and was gone.

I quickly caught the door with my foot and followed him a few steps down the hallway. "Sebastian," I called after his retreated form.

Without turning around, he stuck his fingers in his ears and disappeared around the corner.

I shook my head. What a dork.

Unfortunately, he was a gorgeous dork with a beautiful smile and an extremely tempting proposition.

With another fond shake of my head, I turned to duck back into the room and came up short.

The smile that I hadn't realized crept onto my face flaked off like decade-old paint.

Coach Hansson stood at the end of the hallway, disappointment tattooed across every inch of him.

Coach Hansson pinched the bridge of his nose and squeezed his eyes closed. "You know, Warren. I really wish I hadn't seen that."

"Um—I..."

Coach's eyes snapped up, and he dropped his hand from his face. "No. Don't tell me. I don't want to know. But I am going to give you some advice." Hansson glanced around the empty hallway, walked up to me, and dropped his voice. "Whatever is going on, end it."

"Excuse m—?"

"Only because I want you to focus on your career."

I fought down the indignation rising in me and very deliberately did not yell at my coach. "I am focused on my career. Whatever relationship I have with Sebastian doesn't have anything to do with that. I'm a fantastic goalie."

"Yes, you are."

Wait. What?

"Come with me," he ordered. Once again, I was directed into my meditation room. But instead of being yanked by the Neanderthal that I was sleeping with, Coach Hansson held the door for me and then closed it gently when we were both inside.

Hansson turned to me. "I'm not supposed to tell you this yet, but considering what I just saw, I think you need to factor this into your situation.

The team has decided to keep you on the team past this season."

I must have gone crazy. This could have only been a hallucination. "But what about Hall and Stanton?"

No way would management choose me over one of the Blizzards' veteran goaltenders. I knew when I signed with the Blizzards that I was unlikely to stick around. They already had two record-breaking goalies. Unless…

"Stanton isn't coming back next season. His physical therapy isn't going great, so he's retiring. Hall is coming back next season as our starting goalie. You are going to be our new backup goalie. Management talked it over and your numbers are good. Better than any other goalies your age and with your experience. Plus, as a bonus, ticket sales have gone up since you got traded."

"And Lukin?" I asked, still in a daze.

Coach grimaced. "He's got a bad attitude. And he doesn't block enough pucks to make putting up with him worth it."

Holy shit. I get to stay.

Sure, that was my goal all along, but I knew how much of a long shot it was. I was pretty green, and the Blizzards already had two goalies. But now Stanton was gone, and I felt for him, I truly did; no one wants to be taken out because of an injury. Unfortunately, that was the way of the game sometimes.

Then I snapped back to reality and remembered where this conversation started. "Am I only going to stay if I end things with Kingston?"

Coach sighed. "You know why dating him is a bad idea, right?"

I nodded, but he explained anyway.

"If it got out, you would be dragged through the mud. I'm not saying it's right, but it will happen. And it's not just you and Kingston who would be affected."

"I know. The team dynamics would change, and it could affect the game."

It was the argument I had been giving myself since I kissed Sebastian in that damn elevator. If my relationship with Sebastian came out and the team took it badly, it would be my first game all over again. They would abandon me, and I would be forced to fend for myself. To them, I wouldn't just be a girl playing with them, I would be a lying bisexual who liked to screw her teammates. Well, maybe a few of them wouldn't mind that.

"I'm thinking more big picture, Warren."

"What do you mean?"

"How do you think this would impact the inclusion of other women who want to join male sports?"

It took a second to click, and I hung my head.

"Exactly," Coach said. "You think it was hard for you and McCarthy joining the league? Honestly, the lesbian angle was the best way to go, but what about straight women? What would happen for the future of inclusion in sports if

221

there was a history of female players having sex with their teammates?"

He didn't answer his own questions, and he didn't have to. It wouldn't be pretty. "What if that didn't happen, though? What if no one cared?" My voice was weak, heavy with all the doubt running through my head.

"I can't take that chance."

"What?"

"I have a granddaughter, Warren. She's fifteen, and the best damn pitcher on her high school team."

"Baseball?"

He waved a hand through the air. "I know, I know. I tried to slap some skates on her, but she hates the ice."

"And you think she can make it to the MLB?"

Coach's chest puffed up. "I know she can."

Despite the circumstance, my heart warmed. My parents got the same looks on their faces when they bragged about me to their friends. Since I was a little kid, swimming in my goalie pads, they knew that I would go to the NHL and did everything in they could to support me. *God, I miss them.*

And like Coach, if my parents had the power to ease my struggles in the major leagues, they would have done it in a heartbeat.

Was I ready to risk the career that was drowning in my blood, sweat, and tears for Sebastian Kingston?

I collapsed against the wall and looked around the room with contempt. So much for the calm room I meditated in. It was probably filled with bad juju now. I wanted to drive my fist through the wall and tear down the memories they now held.

Coach looked at me with pity. "Look, I'm your coach, but this is one thing I can't order you to do. It's your career and your decision. So take some time and think on things, Warren. Consider your options and figure out what's important to you."

As if he hadn't just blown up my world, Hansson left me to make the biggest decision of my life.

16

*W*ith a grunt, I slammed the rope to the ground, ignored the pain shooting through my whole body, and did it again. I switched between the two ropes, one in each hand, whipping them up and down until I couldn't breathe. The ropes fell from my shaking grips.

I stumbled and caught myself before I could fall to my knees. My lungs heaved, desperate for oxygen. *Oh, that hurts.*

I flopped down on a weight bench in the empty gym. I felt around on the floor beneath me. *Where...?* I grabbed my water bottle and brought it to my face. The first squirt went into my mouth, the second over my sweat-drenched face. Sweet relief.

It didn't last.

I stood, loosened up my arms, then grabbed the ropes again.

Slam. Slam. Slam. Slam.

"What did rope do to you?" a Russian accent asked.

I dropped the ropes and watched as Lukin entered the Blizzards gym, hands in his pockets. He looked the same, in his team workout gear and a hat, but something seemed off. I studied his face for a second before I realized. He wasn't snarling at me. In fact, his usual cocky attitude and his "Why is this peasant talking to me" evil eye were completely absent. In their place, slumped shoulders and a downcast gaze made Lukin almost unrecognizable.

Add in the fact that Lukin was voluntarily in the arena outside of mandatory practice, and I was wondering if he had a sadder, harder-working twin.

"What's up?" I asked cautiously.

He responded in Russian. "*Did you hear about Stanton?*"

I switched to Russian also. "*That he's not coming back?*"

"*Yeah. I heard from the team physical therapist. He was talking to a doctor about forwarding his medical information since he wasn't coming back. Do you know if Hall is returning?*"

"*He is, as far as I know.*"

With a sigh that made me want to press the back of my hand against his forehead to see if he was about to drop dead, Lukin sagged against the rack of free weights. "*They're sending me back down, aren't they?*"

I worded my non-answer carefully. *"What makes you say that?"*

"Coach was acting weird. He sat me down and gave me a talk. Said if I wanted to succeed in this league, I have to stop fighting with you and everyone and spend more time practicing and working on my rebounds."

"Yeah, your rebounds do kinda suck." I kept my tone light so he knew I was joking, reverting to chirping when I didn't know what to say.

Lukin hummed and toed the floor.

Admittedly, Lukin was an attractive guy. However, his usual demeanor made it hard to see his handsome Russian features. Now, with his soft eyes and shy stance, he seemed almost cute. Almost.

"They're keeping you on, right? I would. You have better numbers than me."

For once in my life, I kept quiet.

His gaze went hazy as if looking out somewhere far, or looking in, before it snapped back to me. I almost took a step back. A determination had filled him, and I was suddenly looking at the immovable wall that was a professional hockey goaltender.

"I want to stay in the NHL. This is what I've been working for my whole life, but I got sidetracked. I got distracted, and I stopped working. I thought I had already made it. Thought I could take it easy since I was called up. But it's harder than ever. I need to stop going out and cut back on the drinking and the partying. I can't afford

to be distracted. Not when taking my eye off the puck for even a second will let it slip through my five-hole."

He may as well have hit me over the head with a two-by-four. "Wow. Coach pulled your head out of your ass."

I barely realized I slipped back into English. Not when my mind was suddenly in the stratosphere. It was like the world was opening in front of me. The answer that I had spent all morning searching for, working my body to the point of exhaustion to try to find some clarity, was startling clear. It had always been. I had just been avoiding it, but I couldn't anymore.

Lukin was talking, his face lightening up as he went on. I tuned back in.

"*...So, do you mind if I join you? Maybe we can go over some drills on the ice later?*"

I absent-mindedly gathered my things, moving toward to door. "I would love to, Lukin, but I have to go do something first. I'll be back."

Without another word to a confused Lukin, I was out the door.

I'm going to do this and get it over with. I'm not going to hesitate or doubt myself or change my mind. Then I'm going to be free to focus on training.

I stood on the brake, and my car came to a screeching halt in front of my house.

"Shit," I screamed at my steering wheel. I punched it for good measure then threw my car into park. I practically dove out of the door, desperate for air.

The sharp March air stung my nostrils and stabbed at my brain. The dried sweat soaking my muscle tank froze against me. I hadn't bothered to change out of my workout gear or take a shower. I'd just grabbed my backpack and keys and took off.

All at once, the thing I was rushing to get done was right in front of me. My chest heaved.

I wanted to pace. I wanted a tennis ball to throw at a wall.

Instead, I walked to Sebastian's house, the weight of my decision crushing me further with every step. The cool afternoon air steadily lost its refreshing feel until my face was left feeling raw. I forced myself to keep on going.

Both too quickly and way too soon, I found myself standing outside of Sebastian's house. The short walk hadn't calmed me any, but I refused to fuck about on the sidewalk. I had made up my mind. I shoved steel into my spine and went right up to his door. With a shaky hand, I reached for the handle, found it unlocked, and stepped inside.

The wind picked up the door and slammed it closed behind me. I couldn't hold back my flinch.

228

"That you, Riles?" came Sebastian's voice. It sounded like he was in the living room.

"Y-yeah."

"I was hoping you would come by. I'm over here. I'm watching game footage if you want to join. Also, to prove how awesome a boyfriend I would be, I got you a present."

My stomach twisted as I shuffled farther into the house and found him lounging on his couch.

He was in his comfy Blizzard-branded sweats, a water bottle wedged between his thighs and munching on something covered in chocolate. I moved around the edge of the couch and saw a pile of miniature Twix bars sitting on the coffee table. A tiny mountain of wrappers was growing on the couch next to Sebastian.

"You were totally right. These are the best chocolate bars. I don't know why I ever thought differently."

My voice shattered into a million pieces, joining the broken shards inside my chest. "It's the c-cookie. W-why would anyone choose a chocolate bar with a w-wafer when you could have a chocolate-and-caramel-covered cookie?"

He popped the last of the candy bar into his mouth and sat up to get his first proper look at me. The bright smile faded from his face like someone turned down his dimmer. "You okay, Riles?"

I sat down on the end of the couch, keeping two cushion lengths between us, and looked at him. "My parents are dead."

He blinked and sat up fully, giving me his undivided attention.

I didn't necessarily want to share this next part with him. The only people I talked to about this were Drew, Mason, and my parents' headstone. But Sebastian deserved an explanation.

I drew in a breath.

"I've never told you how they died, have I?"

"No." His voice was soft, his eyes searching.

"It was a plane crash. They worked at the same law firm and sometimes on the same cases. It wasn't super common, but occasionally they would have to leave town for work. That week they had been in Chicago to help seal the deal on some merger. They should have stayed another day, but the second the signatures were dry, they were on their firm's private plane headed back home." I breathed out a huge stream of air, holding back the tears trying to escape. "They wanted to make it back in time for my first high school championship game."

His face melted into sympathy, and he scooted toward me. "Riley."

I held up a hand and continued before he could, already guessing what he was going to say. "I don't blame myself, and I don't blame hockey. At least, not anymore. It was just a shitty thing that happened. It took me years of therapy to understand that, but I'm in a good place now. I've accepted it."

"But you still miss them."

I sniffled. "With everything that I have."

"I'm so sorry, sweetheart."

Jesus. I didn't think that I could hurt more while talking about this subject, but knowing what was coming was agony.

"The thing is, I was on the phone with them right before they boarded. They were really excited for my game. It was kind of rare, and I was so stoked to have them watching."

"I thought they loved hockey?"

"They did, but they were both lawyers. They didn't always have the time to come to all my games, but they were going to make it to this one. It was the beginning of my career. I was only fifteen, but I already knew I was serious about hockey. I was ready to get into juniors' hockey the next year. My mother and father had stayed up with me for weeks curating a list of teams and organizations. They even made preemptive spreadsheets on all the coaches so they were prepared if anyone refused me because of my gender. I was determined to go all the way in this sport, and my parents knew I could do it. It was all they wanted for me. And I did it. I made it to the NHL."

A weird look flashed over Sebastian's face. "I'm sure that's not all they wanted for you."

"I told you how intense they were about my career. They were basically my agents since I decided I wanted to be in the NHL. Hell, after they died, I found whole files about my games and coaches and my future career projections. They practically made it their life's mission to get

231

me to the big show. And it's my mission too—one that's not over just because I got here. I also have to stay here. I need to focus on my job, Sebastian. I can't have any distractions."

"Okayyyy." He drew out the word. "What are you saying, Riley?"

Just do it, Warren. Rip off the band-aid.

"We can't do this anymore."

His face turned to stone, gears spinning behind his eyes. "What happened?"

"What?"

"Something must have happened. Yesterday, you were so close to giving this a try. I know I messed up with Glass, but it won't happen again." He slid to the edge of the couch. "Just tell me what happened to trigger this, and I'll fix it."

"No," I yelped and shot off the couch.

If he came to me, if he touched me, I wasn't sure if I could keep my resolve, and I had to. I had to do this.

"Nothing happened. I'm just choosing my career. You should understand that. Hockey is my priority. I'm finally on the ice, and I can't risk losing that. Not even for you."

He pushed off the couch. "Riley—"

I stepped back. Twice. "No. You knew that if this arrangement ever came between my career, I was out. Not only do I not have the time to spare, but if someone found out about us, I would be done for. This is my only option, Sebastian. I'm sorry."

I turned around, not able to stand his face anymore, and headed for the door.

I was just reaching out for the handle when his next words stopped me, his voice directly behind me.

"Please don't go. We can figure something out. I love you."

No. No, please. Oh, God.

The wind left my sails, and my head fell onto the door with a bang. I didn't feel the sting. I only felt Sebastian's arms as they curled around my stomach.

My nails dug into his forearms. It would have been so easy to lean back into his warmth, letting him protect me and take away all my worries.

I savored the feel of him and then pushed on his arms. He didn't fight me, and I escaped his embrace.

"I'm so, so sorry," I muttered into the air. Then I was out the door and down the street before my heart could make me turn back.

Twenty minutes later, I was back at the arena gym, running full tilt on the treadmill until I tasted blood. Then I picked up some free weights and pushed on.

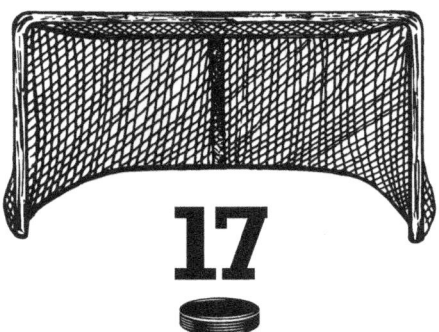

17

*W*ith a heavy thud of my foot, I stopped dead and checked my watch.

New personal best!

With a little pep in my step, I danced up the steps to my house, into the kitchen to grab some water, and through the living room, where my mood was violently murdered.

Like they had been doing for the past few weeks since I broke things off with Sebastian, Drew and Mason sprang out of each other's arms and settled farther apart on my couch. One would think I just walked in on them mid-bone and discovered that they were gay. Honestly, that would have been preferable to what they were actually doing—trying to be "sensitive" about my "break up" by not rubbing their relationship in my face.

I'd told them a million times to knock it off, but they were determined to not cause more pain to my "broken heart." I knew I should appreciate the sentiment, but it was just pissing me off.

Even interacting with Sebastian was less painful than them sometimes. But that was probably because Sebastian hadn't looked in my direction, on or off the ice, even once since he told me he loved me and I rejected him.

My watch picked up the spike in my heart rate.

I took even breaths and watched the number on my wrist go down. This stupid avoidance game was almost over, and then I wouldn't have to see Sebastian again for months. Because tonight was the Blizzards' last game.

I took a distracted sip from my bottle before I realized Drew's mouth was moving.

I lowered my water and removed my earbuds. "Sorry? What were you saying?"

"We came to a decision yesterday and just wanted to give you a heads up."

"A decision about what?"

Mason took over. "I'm going to come out."

A pause, then my mouth dropped open. "Of the closet?"

"Yeah." Mason grasped Drew's hand. "I've been thing about it since that half-naked run-in with Kings—" Mason coughed. "I mean, I've been thinking about it for a while. And I realized that I don't want to have to come up with lame excuses every time I'm seen with Drew. I want to be able to shout that he's my boyfriend. And hold his hand in public. And blow him a kiss through the boards before every game."

Drew blushed.

"But what about hockey?" I asked.

235

"I'm sure it will all be fine. They have queer women in the league." He gestured toward me. "I doubt they will riot over a queer man, and even if they do, I'm tired of hiding. I just want to be out and happy with Drew. I'm willing to take the risk."

Take the risk. Take the risk of ruining his career and losing hockey? Hockey was what made Mason happy. It had been since we were kids. And he was suddenly okay with giving that up? For a man?

Could it be that easy? To just say "fuck it" and throw all caution to the wind?

No, that was impossible. Right?

"Riley?" Drew's voice brought me back to the present. It didn't sound like it was the first time he'd called my name.

The boys were looking at me with concern. I must have been staring through them. I backed up. I hit a wall then corrected my route and reversed farther out of the room.

"That's good," I whispered, not looking at either of them. I nodded to myself. "That's good. You should be happy."

I staggered away and dodged Mason when he stood up to follow me. I was supposed to be celebrating with them. This was about their future, not me. I knew how hard this had to be for Mason; we had been talking about this for years.

He'd never wanted to risk it before, and he had no reason to; he never had a boyfriend before. Especially not one that would have asked him to come out for them. He had never been in love before, but he was now. And he wanted to enjoy life with his love.

I wanted to carve out my heart.

The world swirled.

"Excuse me," I murmured to the air.

When I looked up, I was in my car. I pulled away from the curb and sped toward the rink.

Malcolm, one of the security guys, seemed surprised to see me. That was understandable. It was barely eight in the morning; morning practice wasn't for a couple more hours, the game even further away.

"Warren? This is a little early, even for you," he said from the other side of the metal detector.

"Yeah. I just need to do a few things, Malcolm. Is that all good?"

"Sure." He shrugged and let me through security. I nodded my thanks and went down the hallway, except unlike usual, I turned down a different hall and worked my way up to the upper levels of the arena.

I popped out of the maze at the concessions level. This was where thousands of fans came through to attend our games, and I knew it like the back of my hand. I walked a few sections to the left then headed down the aisle.

Section D, row one, seats four through seven.

It was like the seats lit up the whole arena as I approached them. They were so full of memories, and when I sat down, they all came rushing back. Despite the years I had practically lived in them, or maybe because of them, I didn't remember the first time I sat in these seats. They just always ... were. They were as much a part of my childhood as my favorite stuffed tiger, Lion.

I ran my hands across the cold, blue metal seats. Seat five was mine; Drew would sit to my left, our mom next to him, Dad on my right. Most of the time, my parents would buy a couple more seats for Mason and his mom as well.

You could always find our family at the rink on game days, junk food and homemade signs in hand. Not even work or school could keep us away. My parents always made time for the Blizzards.

It was odd being here without them, looking out on the dimly lit ice that I had actually played on. The rink had lost some of its ethereal quality. It was no longer the place where I saw Quinn score the winning goal of the 2006 Stanley Cup or where Goss blocked a bullet of a shot from Brockovich. At least it wasn't only that place anymore.

It was also where I started my first NHL game. And lost. Where I took a puck to the mask and had my team abandon me. Where I made my friends other than Mason. Where I played my first NHL shutout.

Where I broke the heart of the man I was in love with.

I drew my feet onto the chair and hugged my knees to my chest. The silence of the rink echoed around me.

"Boo," Drew said and dropped down beside me. "Did I scare you?"

"You would have if you hadn't called me five minutes ago to tell the guard to let you in."

"What is his name again?" Drew asked and settled into his seat. It was weird to see him here again. Not a lot of my memories of this place involved Drew; he was never the biggest hockey fan. Or he just wasn't a big fan of coming to the arena all the time.

"Malcolm."

"Right. Malcolm said I was free to stay as long as I wanted."

I hummed.

Drew propped his feet up on the ledge of the glass and folded his arms across his chest. "And I hope that's not too long. This place is kind of creepy when it's empty."

He had a point, but it had already filled up a bit since I got here thirty minutes ago. Staff and vendors wandered around, setting up for the game. Only half of the rink lights were on, casting long shadows across the ice.

"Then why are you here?" I asked. "To be honest, I was expecting Mason."

"He was going to come, but I told him to let me have this one."

"Why is that? You think you can handle me?"

He shrugged and stared out onto the ice. I think it was his first time back in these seats too. He came to all my games that he could, but the tickets I gave him were in a different section across the rink. He could have just bought tickets for these seats if he wanted to, but he never did. I would have seen him if he had. I checked every home game.

There was a faraway look in his eyes. A look I was sure was on my face just a few minutes ago. I stayed quiet and let him think.

Sometimes I forgot how hard Drew had it after our parents died. I wasn't even sure if he had time to process it then. He had come back from college to watch my championship game when the plane crashed. He later told me that the police had called him in the middle of my game, but we had fifteen minutes left until the final buzzer. When it was over and Mason and I were celebrating our big win, he found me.

At first, I was confused. Why did he look so sad? We had won. And where were Mom and Dad? Dad had said they may miss the first period, but they would be there to take us out for food afterward. I hadn't seen them in the stands because I hadn't looked. I was too focused on the game to care about anything else. I just expected them to be there.

It was when I asked Drew where they were that I finally noticed the tears in Drew's eyes. They weren't happy, proud tears; Drew was never one for that many emotions anyway. Behind him, Mason's mom was the exact copy of him— full of pity and heartbreak. I hadn't understood that something bad was happening until Drew motioned me forward then led me away.

Mason had moved to follow us, but his mom grabbed onto his arm, giving us privacy.

In a barely hidden corner off the path of the main locker room hallway, Drew told me about our parents. My cries had echoed through the halls, clashing with the cheers of my team farther in the arena, as I collapsed in Drew's arms.

I didn't remember much of what happened after. Only that Mason's mom drove us home, not wanting Drew behind the wheel. I cuddled into Drew in the back seat while Mason constantly peeked back at us from the passenger's seat, tears running silently down his face.

While I spent the next couple weeks sobbing in my room, Drew didn't have that luxury. He had a funeral to plan. Our family lawyer tried to help, but some things Drew felt he had to do himself, like raise me. Drew was still a kid himself and everyone was telling him I would be better off with an adult. Mason's mom was ready to take me in a heartbeat, but Drew refused.

So for the last of my teenage years, Drew was my guardian. He was a full-time student while having to deal with me, an ungrateful teenager who didn't understand what he was doing for me and what he was giving up.

It was only when I moved away for hockey training and lived alone for a few months that I realized all the things he didn't have to do.

For all his tough-guy exterior, Drew was the most compassionate person I'd ever known.

"You're kind of an idiot, Riles."

"W-what the fuck? Why?"

His head flopped to the side, making lazy eye contact, and he regarded me with fond irritation.

"Why are you so determined to give up everything for this game? What's the point?"

I gaped at him. "How could you ask that? Mom and Dad wanted me to be the best hockey player I could be. You know, it was the last thing they told me. 'We'll be there soon, Riley. Be the best you can be.'"

"And you can't be a great hockey player and have a love life? Because I'm sure that there are quite a few players that would strongly disagree with you."

"Sure, but none of them are dating a teammate."

Drew inclined his head in acquiescence. "True."

"I can't let anything threaten my career. I have to be the best."

"Why? Does being the best make you happy?"

"Of course. I wanted to be the best NHL goalie since the first time I strapped on pads and stopped my first puck."

He chuckled. "I know. You ran around the house in full pads and told everyone to bean you with tennis balls."

It was awesome practice. It took me a few bruises to the face, but I learned how to catch speeding projectiles very quickly. "You always threw them the hardest," I grumbled then got back on track. "Most parents would have just humored me. I mean, what were the chances that I would make it into the NHL as a woman? But they fought for me."

There were no women in the league at the time, and the idea that there one day would be was just preposterous. That didn't stop my parents.

"So, you think you owe it to them?" Drew asked as if the very idea was crazy.

I was just as perplexed as he was. "Of course."

Drew took a deep breath. "I've got to tell you something, Riley."

That didn't sound good. I braced.

"Mom and Dad didn't give a shit if you made it to the NHL."

I blinked. What did that even mean? Of course, they did. Drew knew how much time and money our parents spent on hockey for me. Sure, our family was wealthy, but you didn't just throw that kind of money around if you don't expect results. That's not fiscally responsible, and our parents were both corporate lawyers who grew up poor. They didn't throw around money unnecessarily.

I was obviously not computing, so Drew went on. "They were never pressuring you. Hell, did you ever see them pressure me to go to college?"

I paused. They must have. Our parents wanted us to succeed in life. That was their only demand of us. But … no. They never pushed Drew to go to college or even told him what to major in like many other parents did with their children.

"They didn't care what we did with our lives, Riles. They just wanted us to be happy. Being my own man is what made me happy. And you? You were all about hockey. So they made damn sure we had everything we needed in life to get where we wanted to go. But they would have done the same thing if you had wanted to be a professional line dancer. Or scuba diver. Or a-fucking-brain surgeon. It never mattered. They just wanted us to be happy."

I slapped a hand over my mouth. *Oh, God.*

All at once, my world flipped inside out, and I could see every decision I'd ever made as if I was looking at someone else.

"Now I have to ask you something, Riley. Are you happy?"

My chest heaved, and a sob built up in my throat.

"Are you happy? Could you die today and not have a single regret?"

I think he already knew the answer to that. Unfortunately, so did I. I had known for months what I wouldn't allow myself to admit out loud.

My body fell forward into Drew. and he wrapped me up in his arms. Buried in his chest, I shook my head.

I gave in. "No."

He rubbed my back as I processed, then broke the silence after a few minutes of my silent heaving. "Are you happy with him?"

I sniffled. "Yes, but it's not that simple."

"Is this about Mason coming out? Are you not ready for the world to know the truth about you?"

"No. I would come out in a heartbeat for him. It's the fact that he's my teammate. Do you know how bad that would be? What people would say?"

Drew pulled back abruptly and took my face between his hands roughly. His eyes bore into mine. "Riley, if you really want to give Mom and Dad their last wish ... be happy. Chase what you love, and screw anybody who says you can't have it. You're Riley freaking Warren, daughter of Alina and Martin Warren. Nothing can stop you. Especially idiots who don't have a fraction of your talent. You've never given up over a little hard work. Don't start now."

God, what did I do to deserve Drew? He wasn't the first person I would call to shoot pucks at me. But he was always the one to come through right before the buzzer.

I pulled myself together and wiped at my face.

"I-I have to go tell him. Now. I don't want to wait another minute. I need to apologize for being an idiot." These past weeks had been hell, and I was ready to end it. That was if Sebastian would take me back.

"No."

I stopped mid-rise. "What?"

"It's your last game this season, Riles. Wait until things have calmed down a little."

Right. Right. Okay.

The second the game was over, I was going to his house and getting my boyfriend back.

18

Where the hell is he?

I craned my neck over the crowd in the locker room, searching for the familiar wavy, black helmet of hair. Nothing.

Honestly, I was getting worried at this point. It was only a couple hours before game time, and I hadn't seen Sebastian. He even skipped our last mandatory practice this morning. Even the other players were confused at that. Sebastian "The King" Kingston did not miss mandatory practices. Hell, he rarely missed voluntary practice.

Then, halfway through his speech about just enjoying our last game and having fun, Hansson was called out of practice and off the ice by a guy in a suit that I vaguely recognized. Something was going on.

"Riley!"

My head whipped around as Mason entered the locker room and pushed past a hoard of hockey players. I stood to meet him, searching his face frantically. "What's wrong? What's going on?"

"You need to come with me." Mason took my hand and towed me out the door.

"Mason. Mason!"

He didn't answer and continued to drag me out of the lounge area and took a sharp right.

I dug my heels in. Mason jerked to a stop with me.

"Mason. Tell me what's going on right now." My tone left no room for argument. I was fighting off every instinctual reaction that was telling me someone was dead.

"You need to talk him out of it. He's fucking lost it."

I settled down somewhat. Whatever was going on, it wasn't life and death. "Talk who out of what?"

"Talk Kingston out of ruining his life."

"Huh?"

"He's quitting. Kingston's about to announce that he's retiring."

I was wrong. It *was* life and death.

I took off down the hallway, my sneakers squeaking on the concrete. A second pair of foot-steps joined mine. Mason was on my heels.

It took me seconds to find the crowd by the press room. It was packed with reporters mumbling about Sebastian. I listened carefully to the dozens of overlapping voices.

It was true; the best forward on the east coast was retiring out of the blue. His contract was ending this season, but the Blizzards were guaranteed to renew it in a heartbeat. Except, when they pulled him into our manager's office, he refused to sign the new contract. Everyone wanted to know why.

I knew why. And I needed to stop it.

Thankfully, Sebastian wasn't in the room yet, so I ducked out, Mason right behind me. I didn't have to go far to find Sebastian.

He came from around the corner, moving fast. Coach Hansson was right beside him, keeping pace and talking quietly but quickly. It looked like he was pleading with Sebastian.

I moved forward to intercept them and met Sebastian's stubborn eyes. He froze in the middle of the hall.

Coach spotted me at the same time. "Warren. Thank God. Talk some sense into him."

I opened my mouth to do just that, but Sebastian shook his head.

"No, I've made up my mind. It's been made up for a while," he said.

I stepped closer and lowered my voice. "Sebastian, you don't have to do this. Not for me."

His blank face cracked, and he smiled down at me. "It's okay, Riley. Trust me."

I reached for him, but Sebastian escaped before Coach or I could stop him and was spotted by the press. They parted like the Red Sea before Moses. He strode up to the stage, determination written across every line in his body.

"Is it too late to stop him?" I asked Hansson as Sebastian rounded the podium. The room immediately burst into questions.

"Yes, it is," came a new voice.

We all turned to find Ethan Jones leaning against a wall without a care in the world. He smiled at us and waved as we gaped at him.

"What are you doing here?" I asked him.

"I gotta support my boy."

"How about you tell him not to give up his career for a girl?" Coach suggested.

That was a little harsh, but I couldn't say I disagreed with him.

"Sorry, Coach," Jones said, not sounding it at all.

Coach huffed out a breath and followed Sebastian into the fray. Jones pushed off the wall and stood next to me and Mason. We watched Coach join Sebastian at the pedestal. Sebastian nodded at Hansson. Coach took the mic first and confirmed the rumors of Sebastian's retirement.

I wasn't sure I heard a single word through the roaring in my head. Or maybe that was the roaring of the reporters.

I was twitching to go up there. I didn't think I could forgive myself for Sebastian giving up his career for me. There was no need. Not anymore. I wanted to be with him whether he quit being a hockey player or not. I would gladly take the hit to my career if it meant that Sebastian got to keep playing. I didn't want him to do this out of obligation and then end up resenting me.

"It's okay, Riley. He wants to do this," Jones said.

"He's going to hate me forever." There was nothing I could do now. It was already done. Coach had finished his announcement.

"No, he won't." Jones wrapped his arm around my shoulder fondly. I thought he would have disliked me even more right now. We had been cordial on the ice since I broke up with Sebastian, not even a hint of our budding friendship escaping his cold shoulder. Now, with Sebastian leaving the game, he was acting all buddy-buddy. He should have been pissed, but he wasn't. If anything, he looked relieved.

"Now y'all have a moment to ask Kingston some questions." Coach backed away, and Sebastian took his place.

"Hey, guys." Sebastian smiled at the flashing camera.

I cocked my head to the side. That was Sebastian's genuine smile. The smile that I only saw in private, over dinner, during Mortal Kombat marathons, and in bed. The smile no one ever saw on the ice. And certainly not in a press room.

"I'm only going to take a few questions. I'm sure you can understand that I'm ready to move on with my life outside of hockey. Johnny, I'll give you the first one."

Sebastian leaned on the podium, listening to the question Johnny asked.

I could barely hear a word that he was saying; I was too busy staring at Sebastian in awe. I had never seen him this relaxed in the arena. Or this happy. Usually, from the second he stepped into the stadium he was focused completely on hockey. It was like his determination took him over and he became a hockey robot. But now, he looked ... free.

Before I knew it, Sebastian was stepping down from the podium and heading toward us, snapping me out of my head. Jones pulled him into a manly, back-slapping hug. Camera shutters clicked in a frenzy. Over Jones' shoulder, Sebastian stared at me.

I turned and walked away, knowing he would follow.

This damn room was becoming my sanctuary in the arena. I should get someone to put a name placard on the door. "Riley Warren: she's probably having a mental breakdown." Catchy.

I leaned against the far wall and waited, keeping my eyes down.

It took longer than I expected for the door to squeak open and closed again.

"Sorry. Our team owner pulled me aside for a minute."

"Did he try to talk you out of retiring also?" I still didn't look up at him. I didn't want to face him yet, terrified of what his face would say. He seemed okay before he went up there, but no doubt his decision was finally hitting him full force now.

He snorted. "Yeah. Just like everybody else today."

"Can you blame them?" I whispered miserably and finally looked at him.

He was smiling. "No, I guess not. It was a surprise to most people."

"Not Jones."

Sebastian shrugged.

I waited for his smile to fall and for bitterness to take over his face. He just gave up his career for me. But his smile never faltered, that pure, bright grin permanently affixed to him.

Maybe … maybe he was okay with this. Tentative hope bubbled up in me.

Still… "You didn't have to do this. I was already on my way to beg you to take me back."

His face scrunched in confusion, but he waited for me to continue.

"I know I said I couldn't date you if you were my teammate, but I was wrong. I should have realized earlier that it doesn't matter what the press or anyone else says about us because I love you. I love you and I don't want you to hate me for making you give up hockey. I can't take that."

I watched through slightly watery eyes as his entire face lit up again. Suddenly, he lunged forward and pulled me to him. I happily went.

One hand on my waist, he held my face with his other hockey-mitt of a hand. "Do you mean that?"

I was trapped in his shining eyes and nodded as much as I could with his palm restricting my chin. Then Sebastian's lips were on mine, and I clenched at the front of his sweatshirt, holding him as close to me as I could.

God, I missed this. I missed him.

"I love you too," he whispered against my lips, and the tears I had been holding back finally fell.

I slumped against him and buried my face into the crook of his neck, hiding my wet cheeks. "I'm sorry. I'm so sorry."

He tried to tug me back to look at me, but I clung to him and wiped away my tears on his collar. "About what, sweetheart?"

"I was too late to stop you from retiring." If I had just talked to Drew earlier. If I wasn't so stupid. If I had found him before practice.

"I didn't retire for you, Riley."

I let him tilt my face up. "You didn't?"

Sebastian smiled sheepishly. "Well, a little. But not completely. Not by a longshot."

"T-then why?"

"Because I'm tired, Riles. Tired of hockey, and I have been for a while. I've lost my love for it. If I ever had any for it in the first place."

That didn't make any sense. "What do you mean? You're an amazing player."

He sighed and the scar on his lip puckered. He leaned away slightly, dropping his fingers from my face. I copied him but slid a hand over his chest, down his arm, and grabbed a hold of his forearm, not ready to completely let him go when I just got him back.

"Yeah, I am a good player—"

"Really good," I cut in.

His lips twitched. "Really good. Hell, I was a prodigy from the second I put on skates, but that didn't mean I loved hockey. I mean, sure, I liked it just fine and I had fun when I was playing. But the more pressure that got put on me, the more I just wanted to quit. Except I couldn't. My only friends were my teammates, and my entire life had revolved around hockey for years. I didn't have any other interests, so I just stuck with it."

"And you ended up in the NHL?"

I was astounded. It took a tremendous amount of dedication and passion to make it to the major leagues. Sebastian just rolled on in without the overwhelming passion that all the other players had. Holy shit. The amount of pure talent he had was overwhelming.

"I'm a quick study. With the great coaches I had and all the free ice time at my parents' rink, I practically improved overnight. Before I knew it, I was getting drafted."

Yeah, in the first round. I almost snorted. *Was* a prodigy, my ass. He still was one. If he had the motivation for it, he could have been the best sniper in the damn league. As it was, he was already on his way to the hall of fame. Well … maybe not anymore. I didn't know what his final numbers were. No matter what, his retirement was a loss to all of hockey.

At least I was finally beginning to understand Sebastian more. All his weird pieces were starting to fit together, and I could see him.

"That's why you never became captain!" I realized.

"Yeah. Management kept on offering, but it seemed disrespectful to lead a whole team when I didn't share their love for their game. So I recommended Jones. We were drafted together, and he is just as good as me, but he loves the game. Just as much as you do."

I remembered Jones' smile in the hallway. He was happy for Sebastian. "Jones wasn't surprised that you're retiring. Did he know?"

Sebastian smiled fondly. "Yeah. After our first game together, he invited me out for a drink and asked me why I looked so miserable on the ice. We talked for a while and have been with each other since then. He's my Mason—my best friend and occasional therapist. He was the only one who saw me struggling."

Damnit, I really was shitty at this whole dating thing. I couldn't even tell when my boyfriend was unhappy. "I thought you were just focused. You've smiled a couple times on the ice. At least, I thought you did."

Sebastian took my hands in his, softly playing with my fingers. "I do, but only when I'm with you."

"Really?"

He gazed into my eyes, and I felt the sincerity in every one of his words. "Riley Warren, I've had more fun with you on the ice in the past few months than I've had in my entire career. I never realized how done I was with of all of this until I met you. You've brought me back to life, and I will do anything to keep you by my side. If I knew earlier that leaving this game, that I don't love even a fraction as much as I love you, would have made our lives together easier, I would have retired the second I met you."

I couldn't have stopped the smile on my face if I tried. How could I have been so stupid? I loved this man more than I could have ever loved my freaking career. I would give up everything for this man. There was no competition. I leaned my forehead against his, wrapped my arms around his shoulders, and closed my eyes.

"You okay, Riles?" Sebastian asked after a minute of silence.

I opened my eyes, completely content. "I love you so damn much."

His grey eyes sparkled inches from mine. "I love you too."

We held each other for a long moment, rocking back and forth slightly.

"Okay. Now what?" I asked.

"Huh?"

"What are you going to do now?"

"Ehh. I figured I'd just bum around for a while, eating loads of sugar, not working out, and having sex with my girlfriend."

"Oh. I like that idea." I liked it a lot, but doubt tickled my mind. "Aren't you going to miss hockey though?"

Sebastian hummed. "I guess so. I mean, I don't love it as much as you—I don't think anyone does. But you'll still let me practice with you right?"

"Of course. I'll take any opportunity to kick your ass."

"In your dreams, babe," Sebastian said, then paused for a minute, sobering. "I think it'll be impossible for me to not miss it. Hockey has been my entire life for decades. It's all I know. This will be good for me though. I can finally find something that I'm passionate about. Maybe it's drawing. Or pottery. Or something completely different. I've always wanted to learn how to play the piano. Whatever it is, I'm excited to find it. I've never had a passion before."

I knew he would be amazing at whatever he chose to do. He couldn't not be. He was The King for a reason.

"Other than you, I mean," Sebastian teased, and I had to kiss him for that. He was just too cute.

"Hey! Now we don't have to hide anymore. We can finally go out on a date in public." I was excited just thinking about it. I 'd never had a real relationship before.

"Actually, about that. I think we should wait a little bit before we come out with our relationship and your sexuality," Sebastian hedged.

I cocked my head. "Why?"

He must have caught my doubts because his grip on me tightened. "I just want to make sure there isn't going to be any major backlash on you."

I considered him. "Okay. How do you want to do this?"

"I have a plan! But, first, let's go play our last game together."

I gave his hands one last squeeze then dropped them. "Let's do it!"

Epilogue

Next Season

"*H*eads up, Warren."

I caught the tennis ball heading for my face and glared at the man who chucked it.

"Really, Hall?" I bitched. "I'm trying to focus here."

He rolled his eyes. "Don't be so dramatic. It's not your first time starting. But if you're nervous that you can't live up to my performance last night, I totally understand."

I shook my head.

My new mentor was the weirdest goalie I'd ever met. Which was saying something, because all goalies are weird. We're superstitious loners who like to talk to inanimate objects. Goaltenders' eccentricities were so legendary at this point that they became the new norm. So, when I met Travis Hall when practice began for the new season, I was understandably freaked out. The man didn't have a single pre-game ritual! Not only was that rare for any hockey player, it was unheard of for a goalie.

I honestly wasn't sure if he was real at first. At our first introduction, he said his pre-game routine was "whatever he felt like doing that day." It was the most unathletic thing I'd ever heard. Then I'd glanced down and almost keeled over. Who wore flip flops to the gym?

I was tempted to request a different mentor, and possibly a psych evaluation for him. Unfortunately, despite his weird normalcy, he was also a damn good goalie and was quickly becoming a great friend.

I tossed the ball back to him. "As if, old man. By the time I'm done, no one will even remember your name."

The team was being very careful with Hall since his injury. He was scheduled to rest more during the first couple months of the season to make sure he didn't fuck up his ACL again, which meant I was getting to play more games than most backup goalies. It was the second game of our season, though first on our home ice, and I was more than ready to get back on that ice.

Hall smirked and offered me a hand. "Then get off your ass, Warren. Your fans await."

I let him pull me up out of my locker, then grabbed my gloves and mask. Hall fell back and let me waddle on my skates to the head of the line. As I passed him, I slapped Mason's raised hand. I settled at the front of the lineup and the tunnel to the ice that opened before me.

Behind me, Jones clapped me on my shoulder pads.

"Alright, boys and girl," Jones shouted. "Let's show these guys the might of a Blizzard!"

The team hooted and hollered, our voice refracting off the concrete wall. Then we were off, following the tunnel until we could see the light coming from the end.

We emerged to deafening cheers.

Leading the team around the perimeter of the ice, I soaked in the sounds of the rink. This, right here, was my favorite place.

Well, one of my favorite places.

As if my family's old seats were magnetized, my eyes immediately found section D. Instead of the usual strange faces that sat there, I recognized the occupants. The air left my lungs like I had taken a puck to the ribs.

Drew and Sebastian.

As if he had been watching me since I stepped onto the ice and was just waiting for me to find him, Sebastian met my eyes and smiled. It was the smile that I had seen every day over the off-season. I fought the urge to skate full speed through the plexiglass and into his arms.

I barely reined myself in and gave him a friendly wave, hoping he could see the love in my eyes.

The lines on his temples creased, and he waved back.

Sebastian's big plan had been going very well so far, if a little slow. We were still in stage one—friendship off the ice. The paparazzi probably had dozens of photos of us, some with Mason, Drew, Jones, and the occasional Berg. But more and more, Sebastian and I were being photographed alone together. Still, as far as the world knew, I was a full-blown lesbian.

But that would be changing in a couple days when we started stage two—coming out.

Mason and I were ready to make a splash. Our comments were already written out and everything. I was just glad that we were doing this together. Whatever happened, we wouldn't be alone.

If all went well, stage three would be a breeze. It was also the stage I was most looking forward to. I would finally be able to hold Sebastian's hand in public. Maybe even kiss him. A fluffy feeling shot through my heart, and I only just held in my girlish squeal.

We were so close to our happy ending. I could practically taste it.

On my next lap around the ice, I snagged a puck and plowed to a stop in front of the section D boards.

I tossed the rubber disk up and over the glass to my family.

Book Club Questions

1. There has always been a debate about whether women could, or should, join men's professional sports. What are your thoughts? Could, or will, it eventually happen?

2. Do you think athletes or any other celebrity has an obligation to share their lives with the fans that, to a certain degree, keep them in business? Why or why not?

3. Who was your favorite character in *Love Me, Goaltender*?

4. If you were Sebastian, would you have retired?

5. Why do you think there are not many out queer athletes in this day in age? Is the sports world just behind the curve or is there a bigger issue at hand?

6. Are Twix truly the superior candy bar?

7. What do you think the reaction of hockey fans will be when Riley and Sebastian reach stage three and reveal their relationship?

8. What is your favorite hockey team?

9. Can Lukin be redeemed?

10. Which character's story do you want to see next?

About the Author

Mandy Fate is a new, young author trying to share her love of love with the world. She was born and raised in Houston, Texas with the most caring and supportive parents in the world and with the two most annoying, yet encouraging, big brothers.

Like every author, Mandy grew up with an addiction to books. And there was no cure. Especially when she (at an admittedly too young age) picked up her first romance book. She was hooked.

Now, fresh out of college and bright-eyed, she is wearing out the keys of her laptop with her excitement and ambition to become the author she has always wanted to be.

More books from 4 Horsemen Publications

Romance

ANN SHEPPHIRD
The War Council

EMILY BUNNEY
All or Nothing
All the Way
All Night Long: Novella
All She Needs
Having it All
All at Once
All Together
All for Her

KT BOND
Back to Life
Back to Love
Back at Last

LYNN CHANTALE
The Baker's Touch
Blind Secrets
Broken Lens
Blind Fury
Time Bomb

VIP's Revenge
Chef's Taste

MANDY FATE
Love Me, Goaltender
Captain of My Heart

MIMI FRANCIS
Private Lives
Private Protection
Private Party
Run Away Home
The Professor
Our Two-Week, One-Night Stand

SHAE COON
Bound in Love
Controlling Assets
For His Own Protection
Her Broken Pieces
The Roma's Claim
The Roma's Promise

Discover more at 4HorsemenPublications.com